THE BLOODTHIRSTY BEE

A PROVENCE COZY MYSTERY

ANA T. DREW

JULIE CAVALLO INVESTIGATES

CONTENTS

Chapter 1	1
Chapter 2	11
Chapter 3	20
Chapter 4	28
Chapter 5	38
Chapter 6	44
Chapter 7	52
Chapter 8	61
Chapter 9	68
Chapter 10	76
Chapter 11	83
Chapter 12	89
Chapter 13	95
Chapter 14	103
Chapter 15	111
Chapter 16	118
Chapter 17	124
Chapter 18	130
Chapter 19	137
Chapter 20	144
Chapter 21	151
Chapter 22	155
Chapter 23	164
Chapter 24	173
Chapter 25	180
Chapter 26	186
Chapter 27	192
Chapter 28	198
Chapter 29	204
Chapter 30	212
Chapter 31	219
Author's Note	227

FREE RECIPE BOOK	229
About the Author	231
Also by Ana T. Drew	233

Copyright © 2022 Ana T. Drew

All Rights Reserved.

Editor: Janine Savage

This is a work of fiction.

Names, characters, places and incidents are the product of the author's imagination or are used fictitiously. Any resemblance to actual events, locales, or persons, living or dead, is purely coincidental.

No part of this publication may be reproduced, or transmitted in any form or by any means, electronic or otherwise, without written permission from the author.

CHAPTER 1

A huge swamp-green Easter Bunny waves at me. Despite the urge to flee, I wave back and survey the monster.

Am I looking at a remote-controlled toy manufactured by a color-blind cooperative? Or is the bunny a costume worn by a basketball player standing on stilts? What if it's a machine that hosts a teeny-weeny blobby alien in a command capsule located behind the eyes?

I decide the second one will be my working theory for now.

My friend Salman nudges me in the side. "Is this mall always so bizarre? Or are they marking my inaugural visit?"

"Whenever I shop here, 3 Cicadas is as conventional as a Provence mall can be."

He touches the back of his hand to his forehead, feigning despair. "Julie, I'm telling you, it's the tragedy of my life! Normal is what I seek. Weird is what I get."

Suspecting that this is about his ever-complicated love life, I pat his shoulder while we gaze some more at the dinosaur-sized bunny. As if to reinforce the prehistoric vibe, the creature lifts his front paws, curled, to either side of his chest. If there's indeed a human inside the thing, I bet they're doing it on purpose.

I turn to Salman. "OK, say goodbye to Easter T. rex and let's find that shop you were raving about. I don't have all day."

We skirt around the bunny to the mall map and find the boutique we came here for.

Fifteen minutes, two elevators, and countless aisles later, I emerge from the changing room, decked out in a shimmery mini dress.

Salman eyes me up and down. His expression is deliberately inscrutable, and his lips are sealed.

I swivel around in front of the mirror, twisting my neck to see how the fabric drapes over my derriere. It neither hangs nor stretches, which is good.

"What do you think?" I ask Salman.

He flashes me an enigmatic smile.

I put my hands on my hips. "Will you talk, please?"

"Regardless of what I say, you should trust your own eyes, Julie." He points at my reflection in the mirror. "Hips don't lie."

I scowl. "Seriously? You insisted on coming along to help me pick the right outfit, and this is all you have to say? What kind of friend are you?"

He brushes a hand over his long, wavy mane. "I'm here because the budget you allocated to this purchase was so inadequate. I couldn't let you do this unsupervised."

"You're such a drama queen!"

"Look me in the eye and tell me you knew about the clearance in this boutique." He pins me with a stare. "Tell me you wouldn't have gone to the cheapest retailer instead and paid full price for poor quality."

I lower my gaze. "That's exactly what I would've done."

"So, you acknowledge I saved you from a social disaster?"

"Oh, please." I pull a face. "It's just a high school reunion, not my wedding day."

"High school reunions are more stressful than weddings."

"Have you been wed?"

"No," he concedes.

"I have. My wedding was one of the most stressful events of my life."

"More stressful than your divorce?" he asks slyly.

"No, of course not."

He prowls around me, examining the dress from every possible angle. "On her wedding day, the bride is a princess, an untouchable, the One Everybody Cuts Some Slack."

"I don't know about that…"

"On your wedding day, did you hear anything but compliments? Did anyone say anything mean to you?"

"I don't think so…"

"See?" He stops in front of me, blocking out the mirror. "People don't judge you on your wedding day. Not to your face, anyway."

"While at high school reunions, they do?"

"High school reunions were invented for that specific purpose, *chérie*. It's their raison d'être."

Hmm… "Maybe."

"This dress will do," he declares without the slightest transition. "It isn't glamorous, but it fits in all the strategic places. Given your budget and time constraints, I say go for it."

I return to the changing room. "You were a lot nicer last time we met."

"It was your birthday, silly. What kind of heartless ass would be mean to a friend on such a depressing occasion?"

Ever since Salman moved from Lyon to Avignon, only an hour's drive from Beldoc, I've been seeing a lot more of him. And I love it. Another thing I love is that my pâtisserie has been profitable for months now. Throw into the mix that I've been in a relationship since December, and it will come as no surprise that this year feels like a gift.

I pay for the dress, and we head down the brightly lit central alley toward the food court. If we find a vacant table and get served fast, I can be back in my shop by three-thirty.

Julie's Gluten-Free Delights is closed to customers today, and my two employees are enjoying their second day off. Me, I can only afford a few hours around lunchtime. Being the boss and proprietor of a small business, I can rarely slack off two days in a row, especially not during the Easter chocolate-buying craze.

I detect that the food court is around the next corner before I can see it. My nose senses lemongrass and curry from the Thai joint, garlic and Provençale herbs from the regional counter, and grilled meat with fries from the fast-food place.

Salman and I pick the Thai restaurant.

"How's it going with the boyfriend?" Salman asks after we've placed our orders.

"Good."

He quirks an eyebrow. "More than good, if that smugly happy smile is any indication."

Oops, I didn't realize I was smiling! Things *have* been good between Gabriel and me, both in the bedroom and in other rooms of my little apartment. When he's in town, he comes over after work. Sometimes, we go out to dinner or the movies. But most of the time, we cook and watch a show on my laptop. We talk a lot. And we make love.

He has a small apartment in the gendarmerie barracks not very far from where I live, but I haven't been there.

"Have you met his folks yet?" Salman asks. "It's been, what, four or five months? And what about his friends?"

"I haven't met them yet."

"What about your family?"

"I've only told my sisters about him, but not my dad or my friends."

His thick lashes fly high. "Why ever not?"

"We both feel it's too soon." *Or, at least, that's what I tell myself.*

"But Rose knows, right?"

I roll my eyes. "Rose may've been sixty-five years old for the past decade, and she may even believe it, but no change in her granddaughters' relationship status can escape her notice."

"Your gran is a hoot."

Just as I open my mouth to ask him about his love life, he springs up from his seat. "Quentin? Man, I'm so happy to see you!"

I follow Salman's gaze to a tall, robust man in his forties studying the menu board. He's muscular but not in a way people get when they live in the gym and eat steroids for breakfast, lunch, and dinner. Like Gabriel's, his bulk is of a healthier, evenly distributed variety that comes from a physically active lifestyle spiced up with some weight lifting. He has a clean-shaven face, still youthful despite the receding hairline. His features are regular and inconspicuous. The only thing that stands out is a raised black mole over his right eye in the arch of his eyebrow.

I home in on his brown eyes. There's an aloofness to them, but it vanishes as soon as he recognizes Salman. "*Hé, mon vieux!* What are you doing here?"

"Hanging with a friend." Salman points at me. "And you? Are you alone?"

Quentin nods.

"Join us!" As an afterthought, Salman turns to me. "Do you mind?"

I shake my head. One would have to have the social skills of a Komodo dragon to say "I do, actually" at this point.

Quentin sits down at our table, and Salman informs me that the pair of them go way back, to a physical therapists' convention in Paris some fifteen years ago, where they did more drinking than learning.

A server turns up, and Quentin orders a pad Thai, same as Salman and me.

"Are you a massage therapist like our friend here?" I ask Quentin.

"Close, but not exactly. I'm a chiropractor." He stiffens and glances sideways. "That is to say, I was."

Our food arrives and we dig in.

"So," Salman says to Quentin. "When did you... um... come back?"

I shoot him the side-eye, surprised at my friend's sudden stammer.

Instead of answering his question, Quentin turns to me. "What Salman was trying to ask is, 'When did they release you from prison.' The answer is three months ago."

"Three months?" Salman leans in, looking at once surprised and relieved. "Why didn't you get in touch? Why haven't I bumped into you before? Where have you been hiding?"

"In Dubai."

Salman's head jerks backward. "Dubai? Doing what?"

"I believe Julie here needs some context," Quentin says, bless his considerate heart. "Fifteen months ago, I was convicted of manslaughter and sentenced to a year in jail."

I survey him. "What happened?"

"One of my regulars suffered a stroke following my

treatment. I'd been gentle and careful, as always, and I had nothing to do with her stroke."

"But the judge convicted you…"

"The case officer had recently read an article about a woman who suffered a stroke caused by chiropractic manipulation of her neck," Quentin says. "He became convinced that it was exactly what happened to Coralie Bray, my patient. I went to jail for medical malpractice."

I take that in. "Was there an autopsy done?"

"Yes," Quentin replies.

"What did it show?"

"The findings were inconclusive," Quentin says. "Or, as they put it, nonspecific. I suspect the ME would've exonerated me if it weren't for the pressure from the lead investigator and the magistrate."

"It's scandalous!" Salman interjects.

"If someone performed a second autopsy," Quentin picks up, "and if they looked beyond the evidence of vertebral artery dissection, I believe they'd find something."

I anchor my gaze to his. "Have you asked?"

He gives me a tight, don't-be-naïve smile. "No judge would order an exhumation and a second autopsy at this point just to humor me."

"What if her family asks for it?"

"Coralie didn't have any children, and her parents are dead now," he says. "She had two nephews. They're her deceased sister's sons."

"What if they asked?"

He draws in a shaggy breath. "They won't. They've bought the theory that I caused her death."

Salman grimaces. "When you hear this, you'd think chiropractic malpractice is something common. But it's extremely rare."

"How rare?" I ask.

"Chiropractor-caused strokes are rarer than fatal side effects from a bunch of meds doctors prescribe all the time."

"One in ten million, according to our professional associations," Quentin adds. "Our haters place the risk at one in forty thousand."

"Which is still very rare," Salman points out.

I knit my brows. "But how can some pulling and twisting of the body cause a stroke?"

"If the chiropractor is too aggressive, a tear may form in one or both of the arteries in the back of the neck, which are connected to the brain," Quentin explains. "The artery would then bleed, a clot would form, enter the brain, and cause an immediate or delayed stroke."

"Were you aware of the risk?" I ask him.

"Of course." His mouth paints a humorless, lopsided smile. "I was super careful, and I'd taken malpractice insurance, too."

I stare at him, perplexed. "But then, how did you end up in jail?"

"The case officer, Coralie's nephews, and the prosecutor all argued that I'd never informed her of the risk, and that I had performed her neck adjustments without permission."

"Was that the case?" I ask. "Did you have her permission?"

"Orally."

"When professionals in our line of work have a longtime, trust-based relationship with a client," Salman chimes in, "we sometimes forget to get them to sign a form for every little thing we do."

Quentin nods woefully.

Salman turns to him. "So, what were you doing in Dubai?"

"I'd lost my license, so after my release, I was looking for a new area of work and a fresh start away from here, away from gossip." Quentin points to our plates. "Please, eat before it's cold and unappetizing!"

Salman swathes his fork in rice noodles. "I hear you, man."

"I have green fingers," Quentin says, picking up his chopsticks. "The plan was to become a gardener."

"Did you receive a job offer in Dubai?" I ask him, opting for chopsticks, too.

"Not until two months into my stay."

Salman looks up at him. "Do you enjoy your new occupation? Are you still based in Dubai?"

"No and no."

Salman and I startle at such a clear-cut reply.

"Dubai is very hot... And I bet you made less than as a chiropractor," Salman ventures a guess.

"A lot less," Quentin agrees. "But it's not even that. As a chiropractor, I was helping people. I fixed countless bad backs, sore necks, and aching shoulders. Headaches, too. All sorts of problems caused by misalignment of the joints."

"You rocked at your job," Salman says.

Quentin sets his chopsticks down, chest heaving as he addresses Salman. "You know that feeling when you fix someone? The joy, the satisfaction—"

"Oh yes, and I'm only a massage therapist!" Salman's round-cheeked face glows with sympathy. "You chiropractors can work miracles. You were one such miracle worker."

We spend the next five minutes munching and gulping in silence.

Neither of the men actually said it, but I have the distinct impression they don't think Quentin had had anything to do with Coralie Bray's stroke. My injustice radar is blaring inside my head.

Poor guy!

Now, I do get Coralie's nephews' actions, myself obsessed with bringing to justice the man who caused my mother's death. They needed a culprit because, let's face it, blaming a person is easier than blaming dumb luck. The cops and magistrates gave them what they needed.

But sometimes, there is no culprit. Sometimes, it really is just dumb luck. No ill intentions, or incompetence, or mistakes. No one to blame. No villain in the story.

And casting an innocent man as one is just plain wrong.

CHAPTER 2

Salman, Quentin, and I finish the meal in a lighter atmosphere. The men talk about their common acquaintances. I think about the chores that await me. I have to buy some stuff in the supermarket in the basement, after which Salman will drop me off at the pâtisserie. Normally, I would've come to 3 Cicadas by bus or had Rose drive me here, but he'd insisted on chauffeuring me to show off his new car.

Speaking of Rose, I pull the note with the items she asked me to get from my handbag.

"Your shopping list?" Salman asks.

"Rose's." I turn to Quentin. "My grandmother. I'll just grab the things she needs and then we can go."

Salman extends his hand, palm up. "May I see the list?"

I hand it over.

"Bleach, microfiber cloth, sponge," he reads out. "Heavy-duty scrubbing brush, tear-resistant trash bags."

He opens his eyes wide before crinkling them to slits. I hold his gaze, silently defying him to go down that route.

But that's precisely where he goes, "I'm assuming she already owns a bone saw and a spade?"

If it weren't for Quentin's presence, I would've said, *And they came in very handy.*

"It's for her Big Spring Clean," I say with a deliberate weariness to my voice.

"Of course." Salman returns the note. "Off topic, but what happened to Rose's charming boyfriend, the notary? I didn't see him at Rose's big soirée last month..."

"She broke up with Serge last November."

"Shame," Salman says. "I liked him."

"She liked him, too." In response to Salman's puzzled look, I just say, "Long story."

Five minutes later, the three of us are out of the food court, heading to the elevators.

Salman turns to Quentin, "Hey, are you busy this afternoon?"

"No, why?"

"I'm free, too. We could drop Julie off at her shop and go for a beer or something. I want to hear all about Dubai."

Quentin nods. "Deal. I'd love to catch up."

After I've bought Rose's cleaning supplies, we get into Salman's new car—a cherry red four-seater Peugeot he's ridiculously proud of.

Settling in the front passenger seat, I fasten my seat belt, and we take off.

"Isn't your pâtisserie supposed to be closed on Mondays, like most small shops?" Quentin inquires from the back.

"And so it is," I say.

"But you still need to be there?" he asks, confused.

"Mondays are Julie's bookkeeping days," Salman explains in my stead.

I turn around. "Actually, this Monday is for more than

that. This morning I was at the shop at seven a.m., dressing the windows for Easter."

"Ooh, I want to see that!" Quentin winks. "But I bet it wasn't as exciting as the books. A week's worth of receipts to process, what fun!"

I snarl at him. "Must you rub salt into my wound?"

"Must you do it on Mondays?" Salman asks me. "Mondays are depressing enough. Can't you do it daily, or on Tuesdays, and delegate it to Eric or Flo?"

He glances at Quentin over his shoulder. "Eric is Julie's sous chef, and Florence is her youngest sister who helps her out at the shop."

"Eric has enough work as it is," I say, "and Flo is only there on a part-time basis. No matter how much I wish I could delegate the bookkeeping, it's my cross to bear."

A short time later, Salman pulls up in front of the pâtisserie. The three of us get out of the car.

I thank Salman for his help with buying the dress and then turn to Quentin. "It was great meeting you!"

"May I see your Easter display before we drive off?" he asks.

Beaming, I whip out the remote from my purse and open the roll-down security gate. Last year, I switched to a motorized gate after the shop's original one reached a state that resisted repair. But my budget was too tight for a perforated see-through model, so I got a solid one. Which is to say, one cannot see my beautiful window display from the outside.

I've regretted my thriftiness since then. As Rose likes to say, "Cheapskates end up paying twice."

Salman and Quentin step closer to the window and marvel, open-mouthed, at my Easter extravaganza.

In the center, I've placed nest-shaped baskets with chocolate eggs of various sizes and colors. I'm particularly proud of the gold and emerald hues, but also of their rich, buttery flavor.

Around the egg nests, I have a wild menagerie that includes chocolate hens, bunnies, turtles, donkeys, fish, and shells. They all come in three types of chocolate—dark, milk, and white.

And then there are the bells, *évidemment*. What self-respecting French Easter display can go without those magical flying church bells? On Good Friday, they blast off to Rome and then return on Easter Sunday to wheel over gardens and parks, leaving chocolate egg droppings for the kids to hunt for.

"This display is extraordinary," Quentin says. "One of the best I've ever seen."

Eric and I worked overtime every night last week for this, so the praise hits its mark.

I stand taller. "You're being kind."

"No, I mean it."

"I'm a Druze, not a Catholic," Salman says. "So, I've always wondered, why this obsession with eggs at Easter?"

"They symbolize the Resurrection of Jesus," Quentin explains.

"By what mechanism?"

Quentin and I trade an uncertain look. Was it about the rock covering his tomb? Something to do with Lent? With the chicken-and-egg paradox?

The truth is my Catholic family hasn't really practiced since Rose's hippie days back in the sixties. In other words, I'm almost as unschooled in the church dogma as the next Druze.

Embarrassed, I try to wing it, "Eggs are essential to life on earth and in paradise. No eggs, no pastry. No pastry, no joy. I say, we should celebrate eggs all year round!"

The men applaud my impassioned ode to eggs, and we bid each other farewell.

After Salman and Quentin drive off, I go in, lower the security gate, and get down to work.

Some forty minutes into my suffering, there's an assertive rap on the entrance door. The knocker must be someone from my closest circle, because despite the lowered gate and the Closed sign, they know I'm in here.

I grab the remote and open the gate as I walk to the door.

My visitor is not someone I expected to see. It's Magda, a fellow shop owner. My next-door neighbor. My archrival.

We've been at war ever since I moved in. Well, there was a brief cease-fire when she and I, and a bunch of other shop owners and residents of rue de l'Andouillette, ganged up against the mayor of Beldoc, Victor Jacquet. Rose, who at the time was running for mayor, joined us. She lost her bid.

Fortunately, Victor caved to rue de l'Andouillette.

Trouble is, the moment that happened, my reprieve was over. Magda, as keen as ever to extend her shop by swallowing mine, went back to hating me because I refuse to go bust and sell.

I greet her politely as she sweeps past me, her long, diva-like gown swishing around her plump form. As always, she's wearing generous amounts of makeup and perfume, and as always, she reeks of cigarette smoke. The unusual part is that her gray roots are showing. This is the first time in two years that I'm seeing Magda's roots.

She spins around. "I've been restless."

Hence the roots, I guess. "Are you all right?"

"I have a proposition."

"Listen, even if you raise by ten grand, I'm not—"

"It's not that."

I shut up and wait for her to explain what it is.

She moves her lips silently for a few seconds, as if finding it difficult to utter what she came here to say.

"Yes?" I prompt.

"How about we each buy half of Tatiana's?"

I stare at her, speechless. Is she really proposing that we bury the hatchet and become business associates?

"You know that the bistro across the street is for sale, right?" she asks.

"Of course, I do. It's been for sale for months now."

Tatiana, the owner of the run-down eatery, had been having financial difficulties and losing customers ever since I moved back to Beldoc two years ago. Last fall she threw in the towel. The price she's asking is fair, but the bistro being sizable, and the times uncertain, no one is rushing to buy it.

Magda cocks her head. "What say you?"

"Erm…"

"We buy, split, and extend our respective shops." She appears to struggle with the next bit, "Now that your business is thriving, you should look to grow."

"I'm happy with the space I have."

"For now, maybe. But you should think strategically and plan ahead."

"Wouldn't that purchase be an administrative nightmare, anyway?" I ask, looking for a polite exit. "Converting a restaurant into retail space and dividing it up into two separate shops would involve too many impossible-to-get permissions."

"That's what I assumed, too." Magda's lip curls. "This is France, after all, a land where the world's largest herds of wild bureaucrats roam free."

"My point precisely!"

"But I talked to Tatiana, to the building manager, the condo, and the mayor's office. Nobody likes having a dead restaurant on rue de l'Andouillette in the heart of the historic center. They looked at my idea with an open mind. The permits shouldn't be a problem."

"What about the conflict we had with Mayor Jacquet?"

"Water under the bridge." She fixes me with a sharp gaze. "So? Are you in?"

"I'm not."

"Why not?"

"Because I have no money for that acquisition, no need for it, and frankly, no desire," I blurt, abandoning the diplomatic approach.

She responds with a displeased pout.

I cross my arms. "Why don't you buy the whole thing?"

"It's too expensive for me, and I only need half of that space." Too peeved to say goodbye, she stalks out.

I brew more coffee and go back to my receipts.

After the last one is dealt with, it's almost seven p.m. Time to head to Rose's. I'm going to deliver her cleaning supplies and check on the stiff neck she had this morning. Rose is a lifetime yogini and a former PE teacher who takes pride in the great shape she's in. Consequently, every time she wakes up with a stiff neck is as much a blow to her ego as it is to her physical comfort.

In principle, tonight's doga class she's teaching is canceled, unless her neck got better by midafternoon. Rose is the only doga instructor in Beldoc and the surrounding villages. Her following of humans and canines is small but extremely loyal. They swear by her class. The only one who dropped out this past year was her boyfriend, Serge, but that's only because she dumped him.

Speaking of boyfriends, Gabriel is working the night shift, so I may sleep over at Rose's. And we'll binge-watch our favorite Brazilian telenovela, *Passions Burn Bright on the Fazenda*.

Just as I'm about to exit the shop, my phone rings.

"I had a drink with Quentin, and I'm seething," Salman informs me. "The system fucked up his life so bad!"

"It's terrible what happened to him."

"If only he could find a way to prove that it wasn't his fault!" Salman exhales before adding, "If only *someone* could help him clear his name, then he'd be able to recover his chiropractor license."

That *someone* is me, obviously.

"It's been a year and a half since his patient died," I point out.

"I know, but you and your team, you're really good!"

"Flattery won't get you what you want."

"I beg to disagree."

"Where did it happen?" I ask.

"In Arles, which is, what, a twenty-minute walk from Beldoc?"

"Twenty-minute ride."

"That's what I said."

No it isn't, but I won't insist. Salman's transparent attempts to twist my arm don't bother me, in fact. If I had a friend in Quentin's situation, I'd be willing to twist as many arms as it took to help him.

"I'll think about it," I hear myself say.

"Thank you so much! I really appreciate your—"

"I didn't say yes, OK? I said I'll think about it. And I'll consult the team. That's all I'm committing to."

"You'll take this case," Salman announces with confidence that takes me aback.

But it really shouldn't.

Salman gets people. He must've figured out something about me that tells him I won't be able to walk away from the injustice done to Quentin.

How annoyingly deterministic!

I'm a big believer in free will, despite my psychic ability

to see snippets of the past. Even my twin sister Cat's ability to see the future can't turn me into a fatalist. Cat herself says that her visions are a *likely* future, never a certain one. The future isn't set in stone.

With that in mind, wouldn't it be a blast to say no to Salman, just to show that my actions can't be predicted?

Because, free will, baby.

CHAPTER 3

When I arrive at Rose's, her garden welcomes me with a unique smell that dominates this place in spring only, and only during a doga class. The smell is a blend of jasmine blossoms and Rose's homemade incense. It pleases me to no end. The next thing that suggests Rose is holding tonight's class is the music wafting from the back of the garden where her patio deck is. She normally plays the sounds of nature or Tibetan monks chanting during the doga class. But this time, it's ABBA.

I lean my bike inside the fence and amble toward the house. A soft evening breeze murmurs through the leaves. Meditation chimes hanging from tree branches sing softly. There's a patter of paws rushing my way. I squat in anticipation. A moment later Rose's King Charles spaniel, Lady, is all over me, panting, wagging, and trying to lick my face.

At last, I reach the deck, peppered by humans and canines. Rose is facing them, clad in her trendy yoga outfit.

She breathes in demonstratively, and then breathes out through her mouth. "Inhale slowly, exhale!"

The class executes. Even the dogs, eerily quiet, seem to be working on their yogic breathing techniques, too.

Rose's neck must've improved this afternoon. Squinting, I observe her graceful posture and her beautiful face, framed by a silver bob so glossy it sparkles in the soft light of the setting sun.

Yet, something feels off.

There's a vaguely robotic vibe to the way she surveys the class, pivoting her shoulders along with her head. As for the look in her eyes, it's way too spacey, even for her.

Yeah, hmm, no. I don't think her neck got better. She chose a third path between suffering through the class and canceling it. She took painkillers. Or weed. Or wine. Or any combination thereof.

As Rose corrects her students' planks and cobras and guides their sun salutation, my gaze travels between the humans and the dogs. It's the usual crowd, plus one newbie, and minus Serge. Come to think of it, Rose's stiff neck may be due to a suppressed lovesickness. Didn't she tell me she had a particularly bad case of it in the wake of Grandpa's passing?

When everyone is back up from the downward dog, Sarah, Rose's bestie, and Marie-Jo Barral, editor in chief of *Beldoc Live*, notice me and wave. I wave back.

"Bring your arms above your head," Rose commands as everyone arranges their bodies into a new posture. "Palms together, look at your thumbs. Warrior I."

From there, she guides them into warrior II. But she skips that posture. No doubt because it involves turning her head.

A Chihuahua launches into a hysterical high-pitched

bark. Maybe she's a pacifist that doesn't like the warrior sequence.

The new girl breaks posture to cuddle the dog. "I'm so sorry," she says, looking around sheepishly.

Rose flashes her a reassuring smile. "No worries, it's her first class. Just remember to bring treats next time so that you can reward her when she's quiet."

The woman nods.

"About next time," Rose says with a sudden sparkle in her eyes. "Shall we try Drunk Yoga?"

In response to the stunned silence that follows, she exclaims, "It's an actual thing, I promise! All the rage in New York."

A smothered giggle is all she gets from her students

But Rose doesn't give up. "Trust me, it can be extremely liberating if you're in the right state of mind. I speak from experience."

I bet you do! A very recent experience, as in right now.

Marie-Jo raises her hand. "I may try it at home. Or in New York. But there's no way I'm doing Drunk Yoga in public in my hometown."

"Me neither," Sarah and most of the students say.

Rose mouths something to Sarah. If I read her lips correctly, it's "traitor."

To the rest of the group, she pouts and adds, "Your loss."

They do a few more sequences before stretching out on their backs in the corpse pose. The dogs love this pose the most because they can lick their humans wherever they please. While most go for the faces, Lady focuses on Rose's toes.

After a few minutes of this, Rose sits up, crosses her legs, joins her palms in front of her chest, and thanks everyone for doing a great job. With a final *ohm* and *namaste*, the class ends.

Sarah, Marie-Jo, and I corner Rose.

"Is your neck better?" I ask.

Rose ignores my question.

Marie-Jo eyes her narrowly. "Drunk Yoga, huh?"

Sarah shakes her head. "You should've canceled."

"What did you take before class?" I ask. "And how many?"

Rose pats my cheek. "You don't want to know, darling. And it wasn't many, I promise."

"But why?" Marie-Jo purses her lips with tacit disapproval. "You should've canceled the class and sought help."

Rose waves off her friend's concern. "It's just a pinched nerve. It'll be on the mend tomorrow."

"I'm going to check on you tomorrow morning," Sarah says before calling out to Baxter, her pug. "If you're still in pain, I'll drive you to Arles to see my acupuncturist."

Just as I'm about to suggest she see Salman for a good neck massage, I remember the story of Coralie Bray and her death at Quentin's hand. I don't believe it was his fault, and massage isn't the same as chiropractic adjustments, but I swallow my suggestion, nonetheless.

When the students and friends are all gone, it's just Rose and me. Then Flo arrives, and she and I put back the deck furniture and head into the house. Rose is in the kitchen, fixing a salad for us. It smells of salmon quiche, one of my favorites. Flo and I set the table on the patio, and Rose comes out with an unopened bottle of wine. Unceremoniously, I grab the wine and take it back to the cellar.

Rose protests for show, but I know she knows she's had enough for today of whatever it is she had.

While we eat, I tell them about Quentin's misfortunes and relay Salman's plea that we look into his case.

Flo begins carefully, "Have you considered the possibility that Quentin did twist that woman's—"

"Coralie Bray," I prompt.

"Coralie Bray's neck too forcefully and caused the stroke?"

"I have," I say. "But given how extremely rare that sort of thing is, how firmly Salman vouched for Quentin, and my own gut feeling, I don't think that's what happened."

"What do you think happened?" Rose asks.

I consider my reply for a moment. "A woman had a stroke and died. Her nephews needed a scapegoat to blame for her death. The cops decided it would be Quentin. His insurance company found a loophole. A good man's life was ruined for no good reason."

Rose leans forward. "What if he killed Coralie on purpose? Have you considered that?"

"Just because you like him," Flo chimes in, "doesn't mean he's incapable of murder."

"Sure," I say. "But what would be his motive? He lost everything and gained nothing from Coralie's death."

"That makes him the perfect hitman!" Flo bursts out. "He may have been hired to kill Coralie."

The three of us fall silent, mulling over Flo's scenario. Implausible as it is, a proper detective wouldn't rule it out offhand.

I reach for a second slice of quiche, a little disappointed at Rose and Flo's lack of enthusiasm for Quentin's case. If they opt out, I won't take it on. If Eric decides to sit this one out, I won't investigate it, either. All our previous cases were a success because we worked as a team. There's a reason our crew's name, FERJ, is a four-letter word. Remove Florence, Eric or Rose, and Julie is useless.

The bell at the gate chimes. Rose rushes across the garden and returns with someone I didn't expect to see. It's

Igor Lobov, the exuberant handlebar-mustached man from Eau de Provence that Rose and I met at the Chateau d'Auzon a year ago. He and Rose stayed in touch. They appreciate each other's conversation and sense of humor. Igor, in his mid-fifties, was dating the much younger Malvina when we met. I don't know if they're still together.

Igor greets Flo and me warmly before glancing at the table. "I'm so sorry to intrude like this on a family dinner! I was just driving by and thought I'd say hi to Rose."

"What a great idea!" she cries out.

He turns to her. "I tried to call first, but you didn't pick up. So, I rang the bell instead."

She slaps her forehead. "My phone must be still in silent mode! I forgot to change it back after the doga class."

"Well, um…" He smiles sheepishly. "I'll leave you to your dinner then. Sorry for the interruption, ladies!"

He begins to retreat but Rose blocks his way. "You're staying."

"I can't—"

"But you will, because I'll make you," Rose threatens him.

"There's a second quiche in the oven, and we have plenty of salad," I say helpfully.

Flo points to a chair, and Igor plonks himself into it.

With his resistance broken, we set a place for him. I get the quiche. Rose fetches a bottle of rosé and pours him a glass.

Over the next thirty minutes, he hears all about her stiff neck, and the doga class she pulled off in that state. And then, his tongue loosens with his second glass of wine, and he tells us about his own troubles.

His relationship with Malvina is in a crisis. He's lost most of his friends. As if that wasn't enough, his bank accounts, both private and business, are frozen while "the competent authorities" do background checks.

He told his bank he's squeaky clean and has been living in France for decades. But he was born in Moscow. And his business importing Russian delicacies involves frequent trips to, well, Russia. Or, rather, *involved*. It's as good as dead now.

While he downs his third glass, we comfort him the best we can, and tell him it will all sort itself out eventually.

Staring off into the distance, he strokes his spectacular mustache. "Want to know what hurt me most?"

"Losing your business?" I venture.

"That too, but the worst blow was when they kicked me out of the International Beard and Mustache Association." He snivels. "I was the chairman of the Provence Chapter!"

Swearing profusely, Rose reaches for the *rosé* to fill her glass.

I snatch it from her. "Uh-uh. Not tonight!"

"How do you manage, with your accounts frozen?" Flo asks Igor.

"I grew up under Communism," he says. "Expecting the worst from the government is one of my basic assumptions."

My curiosity piqued, I lean in. "You had a secret offshore account!"

"You had a shitload of Bitcoin," Flo tries.

"The old Luddite that I am mistrusts technology, too, and everything digital," Igor says.

Rose takes her turn at guessing, "Malvina lent you money. It poisoned things between you, and that's why your relationship is on the rocks now."

Ha-ha, she's basically describing what happened between her and Serge. With the notable difference that she couldn't bear the thought of Serge's loan poisoning their relationship, so she dumped him preemptively.

"I never asked Malvina or anyone to lend me money," Igor says.

An image of Karl flashes in my mind. "Oh my God, you bummed money off strangers!"

"It didn't come to that." He gives me a sad little smile. "I'd kept some cash in my mattress. I also had a few bobbles like a Rolex watch that I was able to pawn."

We give him a round of applause for his resourcefulness.

Narrowing his eyes, he looks from Flo to me to Rose, as if something wasn't adding up.

"What is it?" Rose asks him.

"I'm just…" He hesitates. "I didn't expect you to be so kind and understanding. Most of my friends weren't. Malvina isn't."

Rose puts her chin up. "I don't trust the government, either. Any government."

"You're a former hippie," I remind her. "Counterculture runs in your veins."

"As do conspiracy theories," Flo adds with a wink.

"What you call a conspiracy," Rose says, "I call resisting conformity. Humanity needs people like Igor and me."

Flo shoots her a defiant look. "What for? What's your unique contribution?"

"We don't follow orders blindly," Rose claims. "We're the ones that keep humanity both from self-destructing and from losing its soul."

"No less?" Flo teases her.

Rose folds her arms across her chest. "No less."

I think I know what she means. It's a moral imperative to be kind to an innocent person that society shoved into a pillory. Or, in my case, to help an innocent person that society pronounced guilty.

CHAPTER 4

It's been two days since I met with Salman at the mall. Rose's neck has much improved. Business has been good. More than good, actually. On this Holy Week, my pâtisserie has been getting a nonstop flow of customers, both locals and tourists. They enter the shop smiling, primed by the mouthwatering chocolate show on display in the window.

My festive Easter creations being on the expensive side, some of the customers hesitated yesterday. After a quick brainstorm with my sous chef last night, we arrived early this morning and spent a solid hour in the lab, making full-sheet pastries for free samples. Once ready and cooled, we sliced them into morsels before transferring each one into a tiny paper muffin cup.

The investment of time and money has already paid off because we sold more by five p.m. today than all day yesterday.

As much as I love being this busy and making money, it bothers me that FERJ hasn't had a chance to discuss Quentin's case again. We all agree that what happened to him was unfair. But everyone feels there's nothing we can do to fix that. *Everyone but me.*

On Monday night after Igor left, Rose, Flo and I spent the rest of the evening discussing Quentin. The planned binge-watching of *Fazenda Passions* was canceled, the main reason being my policy to never watch a soap with Florence Cavallo. Every improbable plot twist and every closeup of a character staring into the camera prompts snark to pour from her and it's more than I can handle. And I can handle a lot.

Flo and I both ended up sleeping over, partly because it was too late and partly to keep an eye on Rose. Needless to say, I didn't sleep well. When it wasn't Rose tossing, turning or going to the bathroom, it was Flo's unintelligible talking and screaming in her sleep. She was having one of her deep, protracted nightmares that started after the beach house explosion and Mom's death.

Today, Eric and Flo swapped shifts because my sister had a lecture this afternoon she couldn't miss. A year from now, Flo will get her degree in art history. Once she has it, she'll be looking for a job in an auction house, a gallery, or a museum. She'll probably quit her part-time gig at the pâtisserie and maybe her own business, too. The tour company she launched with her boyfriend Tino two years back is still struggling, despite their popular Van Gogh tour. Their problem is that every Provence operator offers a Van Gogh tour.

By the time the clock strikes eight, I'm exhausted. Eric hangs the Closed sign. I count our earnings, transfer the money to the safe, and lock both the safe and the till. Eric starts tidying up the front room while I clean up the lab. We're ready to call it a day, when someone knocks on the window. It's Gabriel with a motorbike helmet in the crook of his arm.

Eric lets him in.

"I'm done for today," he says to me when Eric heads to the other end of the room to vacuum the bistro corner.

Like Rose and Flo, my sous chef knows Gabriel and I are seeing each other. Unlike Rose and Flo, he pretends he doesn't, waiting for me to make an official announcement.

"We ride to my place together?" I give Gabriel a wink. "Me, sweating on my velocipede and you, chilling on your motorized horse?"

He grins. "I was hoping to take you to Le Grand Comptoir for dinner first."

"I hope you have a reservation," Eric says, picking up the now silent vacuum cleaner and heading toward us. "It's super full this week. Lea and I were sent away last night."

Gabriel nods at him. "I booked a table for nine."

"Smart move." Eric packs the vacuum cleaner away.

"I have some info regarding Quentin Vernet," Gabriel says to both of us.

Last night, I told him about Salman's plea to investigate the case, and about FERJ's hesitation. I also hinted that it would help us immensely if he could take a look at Coralie Bray's file, in particular the autopsy report, which Salman had described as inconclusive.

"Go on," I spur Gabriel. "We're all ears."

He wags his index finger. "Not so fast. You go first."

"What do you mean?"

"Tell me what you've been able to dig up so far."

I frown. "But I told you we're not sure we'll be taking this case."

He turns to Eric. "What does your boss do when she's unsure about something or other?"

"She gathers as much info about that thing as possible," Eric replies without a moment's hesitation.

Gabriel shifts his gaze to me. "Exactly."

THE BLOODTHIRSTY BEE

"Fine," I say with a shrug. "It isn't much, and you probably already know all of it from the file. We confirmed she had no other family except for her nephews like Quentin had said. She'd recently retired from a lifelong career as a personal assistant for pharma companies, the last one being a start-up in Arles."

Eric completes my report, "We also established that her two grown nephews inherited her house in Pont-de-Pré."

"It's a pretty village halfway between Arles and Beldoc," I add.

"I know," Gabriel says.

Silly me, of course he does. Just because I'm rediscovering the region after fifteen years in Paris, doesn't mean everyone else is as clueless as I am. Gabriel is from Marseilles, but he's been with the Beldoc Gendarmerie for the past five years. Pont-de-Pré may even be under the jurisdiction of his brigade.

"Did Coralie Bray have life insurance?" I ask him, conveniently remembering one of the questions I had. "We couldn't confirm that part through online research."

He raises an eyebrow. "Ah, I see. You already have a theory that her death was somehow caused by her nephews, eager to lay their hands on her money."

"We don't have any theories at this point," Eric denies.

"None whatsoever," I support his claim.

Except, we totally do. Well, maybe not *we*, but *I*, for sure.

"She didn't have a life insurance policy," Gabriel says. "Her nephews didn't have a motive. Her death was an unintended consequence of the treatment by her chiropractor, Quentin Vernet."

"How can you be so certain? Mistakes like that are exceptionally rare!" I prop a hand on my hip. "We did tons of research on that."

Gabriel's gaze tangles with mine. "I'm certain because I

saw the autopsy report. The ME had performed a substance screen. His report doesn't flag anything that would point to the victim ingesting a drug or a poison that would induce a stroke."

"What drug would that be?" I ask.

"It could be an antidepressant mixed with an amphetamine or a diet pill. That deadly combo can cause a hemorrhagic stroke by sending the victim's blood pressure into the stratosphere."

Eric shoots me a "told you so" look before addressing Gabriel, "So we know for sure she hadn't been poisoned."

"I didn't say that."

Eric and I stare at Gabriel, confused.

"I said," he clarifies, "that the ME didn't think so."

I knit my eyebrows. "But then why did Quentin refer to the report as nonspecific?"

"Because you can always run additional, more specific tests," Gabriel explains. "But the ME would need a good reason to justify the higher cost."

I scowl. "He was too happy with the medical malpractice hypothesis to do that."

"Assuming that Quentin didn't make a mistake, then he's a very unlucky guy," Gabriel says. "He was found guilty in the absence of a clear-cut conclusion from the ME. The prosecution must've been very convincing."

The sound of a key turning in the lock draws our attention to the door. Flo comes in, her step light and her face smug. This is the telltale demeanor Florence Cavallo adopts when she has info she knows would interest one of her older sisters.

"In the context of our pre-investigation to determine if we should be investigating," she begins, after greeting everyone, "I have dug up a detail that may be of relevance."

Eric opens a palm. "Do tell!"

He should know better, having worked with Flo over the course of almost two years.

I fold my arms over my chest, waiting for her to name the price.

She shoots him a sweet smile, before turning to me, "I'll tell you if you allow me to advertise our new tour to your customers."

"Fine," I say, "as long as you do it unobtrusively."

She blinks, visibly surprised by my immediate capitulation.

I glance at my watch. "I don't have time for your games tonight."

"Aaah," she draws out, looking from me to Gabriel and then winking at Eric in the most deliberately obnoxious manner. "Oooh! He-he-he! Some people have plaaans for tonight."

"Twenty-four is the new fourteen," I say to Gabriel by way of apology.

"What were you going to tell us?" Eric reminds Flo.

She pulls out her phone. "I did some digging into the social media profiles of our protagonists, and something stood out."

"What?" all of us ask at once.

"Since Coralie Bray's death, her older nephew, Horace Rapp has bought himself a flashy sports car." Swiping at her phone, Flo shows us pix of said car with Horace in or around it.

In some of those pictures, there's a beautiful Asian woman in the passenger seat.

"He also purchased a few overpriced paintings by a young local artist called Yoona Han." Flo swipes back to a photo of Horace and the Asian woman in his bright red convertible. "That's her."

I squint at Flo. "Do you know of her?"

"I had to look her up," Flo admits. "She's French Korean, still relatively unknown. But she was able to open a gallery in Pont-de-Pré nearly two years ago. Art critics see potential in her."

Eric gives Flo a questioning look. "Are you saying this display of wealth makes Horace Rapp suspicious? Was he less extravagant before?"

"Excellent questions!" Flo gives him a thumbs-up. "I am. He was."

I fetch my own phone and open the notes I made when we researched the Rapp brothers' occupations. "Horace is a manager at a company that installs AC units. He must make a decent living."

"And what about Quentin Vernet?" Gabriel asks all of a sudden. "Have you done the same kind of research into him?"

Flo snarls and shakes her head. "Man, that is such a cop question to ask!"

"What do you mean?"

I think he knows what she means, but he won't admit it.

Flo puts her hands on her hips. "Casting doubt on the victim and treating him as a suspect is what I mean."

"The victim in this case is Coralie Bray," he points out. "She died at Quentin Vernet's hand."

Flo holds his gaze. "The victim in *our* case is Quentin Vernet. He was wrongfully accused and convicted for Coralie's death."

"That's our working theory, but we don't know it for certain," I say to Gabriel placatingly before turning to Flo. "Last I checked, you weren't keen on investigating this case."

"I am now!"

Gabriel glances at his watch, then at me. "We have to go."

I motion my sister and my sous chef toward the door.

Once everyone is outside, I lock up.

THE BLOODTHIRSTY BEE

Ten minutes later, Gabriel and I are facing each other across a round bistro table for two at Le Grand Comptoir.

"I advise against spending time on this case," he says. "But if you do, I hope you take every precaution and avoid unnecessary risks."

"Always."

"Ha!" his mouth drops at my brazen lie.

"OK, from now on I will. I promise!"

We place our orders, and then I add, "Besides, this case wouldn't be anything like the previous ones. There's no empowered villain prepared to do anything to protect his dark secrets."

"You can't know that."

"Oh, come on! This case is simply about proving that the system made a mistake, so that an innocent man can get his life back."

"If you say so." He reaches into his pocket. "I have something for you."

As he opens his hand, I stare at an unusual bracelet in his palm. It's made of cobalt blue beads. Each bead has a white circle within the cobalt blue, a smaller turquoise circle in the middle of the white, and a black dot in the center of the turquoise circle.

"Do you like it?" Gabriel asks, his voice anxious.

"It's kind of spooky, but I do." I look up at him. "Truly."

He releases the breath he'd been holding. "I want you to wear it like you wear your watch, from morning till night."

I find myself not only at a loss for words, but unsure how to feel about that statement.

He smiles. "I'm not being possessive or bossy—"

"Um, you totally are."

"OK, maybe a little bossy, but not possessive." He fingers one of the beads. "Does this remind you of something?"

"Yeah, an eye from Hell."

"It's called *evil eye* on the side of the Mediterranean my family hails from."

I frown. "So, you want me to wear a string of evil eyes?"

"They're amulets, in fact. Lucky charms, if you will. They'll protect and reinforce you."

Sitting back, I arch an eyebrow. "Monsieur Gabriel Adinian, a fearless no-nonsense *capitaine* of the national gendarmerie, believes in lucky charms."

He hangs his head in shameful admission.

I knew athletes were superstitious. It appears that law enforcement is, too. At least, the specimen before me. Myself, I don't believe in that sort of thing. That being said, I believe in psychic abilities. Worse, I get vivid visions of murdered people. Not just visions, but entire scenes that I refer to as *snapshots*. Some are trivial, others dramatic. All pounce on me from a past moment that occurred days, months, or years prior to the person's murder.

But Gabriel doesn't know that because I haven't had the nerve to tell him. Maybe I will soon, now that I know he isn't as spotlessly sensible as he appears to be.

I tilt my head to one side. "How come you aren't reinforced by any evil eyes yourself?"

"Who says I'm not?"

"Where?" I give him a brash look.

Mon coco, don't lie to me! I've seen you in your birthday suit too many times to leave room for doubt.

He chuckles softly. "My mother has sewn an evil eye into the inner pocket of every jacket, coat, and pair of pants I own."

"Can they see through the fabric?"

"Indeed, they can. I suppose they have thermo-vision."

"How badass of them!"

He smiles. "May I?"

As I nod, he takes my hand and fastens the bracelet around my wrist.

"You know, I might still choose to refuse the case," I say, knowing he'll be pleased to hear it. "All we've done so far was pre-investigate to decide if it's worth our time."

"Hmm." He doesn't sound convinced.

Nor should he be.

As a detective, he probably knows I'm kidding myself. Once you pre-investigate, you always find things that call for further inquiry. New questions arise. Gray areas appear. Stopping at that point begins to taste like forfeiture, and it only gets worse until it smacks of quitting in the middle of an exciting investigation.

This is to say that Salman will be pleased when I call him tomorrow. As will be Quentin when Salman relays the news.

Flo made up her mind tonight. I have since Monday. Rose and Eric will jump on the bandwagon within days, I can feel it. We're doing this.

CHAPTER 5

The night of my middle school reunion has come. I'll have to suffer through it alone, not so much because Gabriel and I aren't officially an item, but because he was sent to the Alpilles for some emergency tonight.

Smoothing the dress that Salman helped me pick at the mall, I step into the gymnasium of my former school where the reunion is taking place.

The air smells of a wild mix of expensive perfumes. A pleasant buzz of conversation, laughter, and even some off-key singing fill in for a soundtrack until someone at the stereo wakes up to blast hits from twenty years ago.

I look around. In the bright light, men and women dressed to the nines mingle, wearing desperate cheer on their faces. Groups open and close, form and re-form, like patterns in a kaleidoscope. No one ever lets go of their frosty cocktail glass, particularly useful during the awkward lulls. Everyone is side-eyeing everyone, trying to gauge their own social rank in relation to the class average.

I don't blame them. I find myself doing the same thing.

My dress looks fine, and I'm fitter than most. But my hair is home trimmed. Also, my complexion lacks the glow conferred by *institut* treatments, or a good night's sleep. I didn't get either before this event.

All that puts me in the gray zone of mitigated success. In real life, we're the unashamed majority. But at reunions like this, we're the bottom tier, since the worst off rarely have the heart to show up.

What I find a bit unusual about this particular gathering is that it's for former middle school classmates, when high school reunions are the norm. I didn't go to high school in Beldoc, having moved to Paris the year I turned fifteen. I'm a returnee, a *revenant*, as they call the children of *le Midi* who left the old country for an exotic place like Rio, Jakarta or Paris, before coming back home for good.

Now, that doesn't mean I don't recognize anyone.

Quite the opposite, I see many familiar faces. My classmates have changed, but not much. At thirty-two, the women haven't yet filled out. Their faces are still fresh and unaltered by deep lines, fillers, and scalpels. The men have yet to lose their hair and acquire beer bellies visible to the naked eye.

It strikes me that the change we undergo between our late teens and early thirties doesn't show as much as one would expect. We double our years, but the body remains youthful. The maturing happens in the head when it happens at all.

I'm chatting with two women who were my friends in grade six when a guy with a mic invites everyone to approach the table by the wall, under the banner Fundraiser for War Refugees.

Dutifully, I go. A long line forms along the wall. When my turn comes, I proudly give most of the cash I have on me and receive a button to show off.

While I'm struggling to attach the pin to my dress, someone taps my shoulder. "There you are!"

I look up. It's my former classmate Denis Noble.

He'd been out of town for a while, setting up a branch of the family business somewhere. I don't remember where. And I'm still unclear on what the Noble family business is. They weren't wealthy back when Denis and I went to school, which means his parents hit pay dirt during the years I spent in Paris.

Did they come up with a killer concept? Associate themselves with a genius partner that came up with a killer concept? Find a treasure in their backyard?

Anyhow, I was hoping he wouldn't be at this gathering. It's always tricky, not to say awkward, to party with a tenacious suitor you rejected for a guy who'd spent a year and a half feigning indifference.

"Let me help you with that!" Without waiting for my consent, Denis takes the button from me.

My mouth paints a lukewarm smile. "Thanks."

He pinches the fabric of my dress below my collarbone and secures the button. "That's better."

"Thanks!" I say again, more earnestly this time.

"What do you think of my fundraiser?" he asks.

"You sponsored it?" I pucker my mouth to telegraph admiration. "I thought it was whoever organized this reunion."

"Yours truly organized this reunion."

I stare at him. "From abroad? Despite your busy schedule as a successful businessman?"

"What can I say? I'm that efficient."

I perform a demonstrative bow.

"Some of my reasons were selfish," he says. "I wanted to craft an opportunity to spend an evening around you."

Uncomfortable as his admission makes me feel, at least it

explains why this bash deviates from the norm, targeting former middle school and not high school classmates.

"You've been shunning me lately," Denis says. "I had to think outside the box."

"Denis, I'm flattered, but—"

"I don't want to hear your *buts*! This isn't a date, Julie. Let's just enjoy each other's company, as friends." He flashes me a toothy, confident smile. "Deal?"

"Deal." I fidget with my evil eye bracelet. "But I need to tell you something first, just so things are clear between us. I'm seeing someone."

"Who?"

"It doesn't matter."

"I know who it is," he says. "That gendarme, Gabriel Adinian. I saw the two of you on Wednesday, having dinner in Le Grand Comptoir."

I make a point of not denying his inference.

Denis sneers. "It sounds like a *complicated* relationship to me, since you were unwilling to reveal his name."

"It isn't complicated. It's new."

He gives me a slightly patronizing look. "Whatever you say, Julie. And just so you know, I myself am in a new-slash-complicated relationship with Karine."

"The gorgeous heiress to the Prouttes' fortune?"

"The very same. She's been dying to date me since my birthday party a year ago, so I finally caved in."

"You guys make for a dazzling couple," I say.

And I mean it. Both Karine and Denis are rich, worldly, and good-looking. A match made in heaven.

Denis shrugs a whatever. "Just remember I'll be there to pick up the pieces when your fling with the cop is over."

Is he serious? "What about Karine?"

"What about her?"

"She's genuinely into you," I say. "I remember how she

eyed you at that birthday party. Would you up and ditch her for the privilege of consoling the plainer and poorer me?"

"In a wink."

I narrow my eyes at him. This devotion he's demonstrated ever since I returned to Beldoc is so inexplicable it's suspicious.

True, my detective's mind expects everyone to have hidden motives and to lie about them. Also true, I'm more entertaining than the too-slick Karine. And, the story Denis told me about how his dad pursued his mom for years, until she yielded, does help to understand his obstinacy. *But still.*

"What is it," I ask Denis, "that I have that you need so badly you won't give up?"

His eyes dart left and right, and a muscle twitches in his jaw. My question appears to have destabilized him.

As he opens his mouth to say something, a ruckus in the opposite end of the room draws our attention.

Four or five tipsy partygoers are rushing in through the door, laughing and carrying armfuls of thick hardcovers in boring cream jackets.

Did they just raid the school library?

The self-appointed leader of the gang snatches one of the large metal trays from the buffet tables and sets it on the floor. Then he begins to pile the books he brought in, reading out the authors' names: Dostoyevsky, Tolstoy, Solzhenitsyn...

The others follow suit, adding to the pile more Tolstoy and Dostoyevsky, but also Chekhov, Pushkin, and a bunch of lesser known but similarly sounding authors.

I turn to Denis. "What the what?"

He points to the lighter in the gang leader's hands. "I believe they're going to set those books on fire."

"But they can't! We must stop them!"

I take a step in the direction of the imminent auto-da-fé, but Denis catches my hand and pulls me back.

I glare at him. "Come on! We can't let this happen."

"Why not?" He shrugs. "How often do you get a chance to burn a book guilt free?"

"Do you mean it?"

"I do."

I hiss at him, "Let go of me."

"No way." He tightens his grip. "They're too hammered and unpredictable."

I yell at the book burners, "Stop that at once! Have you lost your minds?"

The guy with the lighter freezes up, giving me hope that he's come to his senses. The sheep around him stand still, awaiting his guidance on how to react.

Then he breaks into a drunken laugh and sets fire to the books.

As I watch the pages blacken and go up in smoke, I can't help but think of Igor and what he's recently been through. Then I think of Quentin, who suffered a similar fate, albeit in a different context.

Why do people feel it's OK to punish by association?

I guess it's human nature.

When the real culprits are out of bounds, we settle for accessible surrogates. We go after someone or something near us, preferably someone or something not in a position to defend themselves. An easy target like a Dostoyevsky book. Or like a man with the wrong name and birthplace. Or like a chiropractor with no connections or money to hire a hotshot lawyer.

Once we've pinned down the scapegoat, we point fingers at them. We trash them, fire them, and even imprison them. And then we award ourselves a button for it.

CHAPTER 6

This week, the bookkeeping is being done on Tuesday, given that Monday was all about Easter bunnies, eggs, and church bells.

I've been toiling alone all morning on my balance sheets on this side of the Closed sign at my shop. The unusual part is that, instead of going for a brisk sandwich-munching walk at lunchtime, I plan to eat my *jambon-beurre* in a stationary manner. And not alone, but with Rose, Lady, Eric, Flo.

I mean, we'll be eating separate sandwiches, obviously.

And Lady will be chewing at a fish skin stick.

FERJ is having a working lunch in the riverfront park. It's our first official deliberation of the Quentin Vernet case.

We find a great spot under a weeping willow. Rose unpacks her picnic basket. Flo and I help her spread out a striped blanket. Eric pours everyone some iced tea from Rose's thermos. Lady lays on her belly in a leaf-dappled sunny spot, happy as a clam about her treat. We're all set.

Yet no one takes the initiative to recap what we know, so that we can bounce ideas off each other. Everybody, including me, focuses on their nourishment and environment instead. Rose gazes at the river, Flo contemplates the sky, and Eric stares at his phone.

Watching Lady chew away at her stick, I listen to the midday traffic that the buzzing of insects nearly blots out. As I wolf down my baguette sandwich, several ear-pleasing sounds remind me I'm by the Rhône without having to look at the river. There's the steady chuckle of the current, the oars of a small boat slapping the water, the splashy flapping of wings... The air smells of grass and of a large, clean body of water.

Rose clears her throat. "Before we start talking about the case, there's something I want to throw out there."

Everybody looks at her, intrigued.

She squares her shoulders. "We should charge a fee. We're too good at investigating to do it for free."

"It's our hobby," Flo says. "We do it for kicks."

"And for the pleasure of solving a crime and bringing the perpetrator to justice," I add.

"Why not combine business and pleasure?" Rose looks at Eric for support. "That's what I do when I teach doga."

"Julie and I are pastry chefs, Madame Tassy," Eric says, taking my side. "We can only investigate as amateurs, not professionals."

She turns to me. "For my sake?"

I startle. "Why, Grandma?"

"I need the money."

"But your house is no longer in danger," I argue. "Serge paid off the bank."

"Wasn't his loan interest-free, and deadline free?" Flo asks.

Rose bristles. "It is. But... I miss him. I want him back in my life, you see."

Flo and I stare at her with identical expressions on our faces.

"Then take him back, for pity's sake!" I verbalize the sentiment.

"I can't." She shakes her head. "Not until I've paid him back."

"Of course, you can, Grandma," Flo coos, touching her hand.

I throw my hands up in dismay. "And yet, against everything that's good and satisfying without being illegal or immoral, you won't."

"Don't you see it?" Her pleading gaze travels between Flo and me. "I can't be with a man whom I owe so much money he practically owns me! I'd feel like a courtesan."

"A courtesan, huh?" Flo pouts. "How chic!"

"I was going to use another word, but my good manners stopped me," Rose grunts.

"I'm with you on this one, Madame Tassy," Eric says unexpectedly. "I couldn't be with a woman who owns me, either."

Really, buddy? Given that it was a blood feud and a quest for redemption that led you to your fiancée Lea, I would've sat this one out if I were you.

"Besides, what if we fail to solve Quentin's case?" I say to Rose. "It's cold and offers little purchase. No results, no fee."

Inexplicably, she perks up. "That's the thing! PIs bill for their time and best effort, not a product. That's how Catherine makes a living."

My twin sister Cat makes a living as a professional medium in Paris.

"Mediums don't need a license, but PIs do," Flo says. "We'd be breaking the law if we charge for our investigations."

"How long does it take to get a license?" Rose asks.

I flash a palm. "It doesn't matter. There's no way Quentin is paying for us to have a go at his case. He never even asked me to. It was Salman who did."

"Perhaps Salman would pay…" Rose's voice trails off as she takes in our glares. "Fine, fine. I give up. We'll investigate out of the goodness of our hearts."

"And for the high of solving a case," Flo adds.

"And so that justice can triumph." I brush the breadcrumbs off my lap. "So, let's recap. Based on what we know so far, I propose two working theories."

Rose hurls a bouncy ball for Lady to retrieve. "We're all ears."

"One," I say, "Coralie suffered a stroke due to natural causes. That it happened after her session with Quentin was a tragic coincidence."

Eric scratches his cheek. "In that case, there's no culprit. Our goal will be to show the cause of death was natural."

"The second theory is that someone who stood to profit from Coralie's death had given her poison or drugs to induce a stroke."

Flo wrinkles her nose. "Quentin's misfortune was collateral damage."

"That's right," I say.

Lady returns with the ball, and Rose rubs her behind the ears. "Proving the first theory would be impossible, given the inconclusiveness of the autopsy. I suggest we start with the second one, that Coralie was murdered."

Everybody agrees.

Flo leans in. "Her nephews, Horace and Leon Rapp, should be our primary suspects. Especially, Horace."

"Because of his extravagant car and the paintings?" Eric asks.

We're all in agreement again.

Eric shifts uncomfortably. He has that look on his face I

know well by now, the look that tells me he's about to announce that he ruined a batch of macaron shells or lost a cream cake on the floor or gave a customer the wrong change.

"Don't hit me," he begins, "but if we're being thorough, shouldn't we suspect Quentin, too?"

Ah, I see. The inflammatory idea Gabriel planted the other day has taken root.

"What would be his motive?" I ask calmly.

"Perhaps he lives a double life as a hitman," Flo offers.

I raise a skeptical eyebrow. "He was investigated by the police. They would've spotted something like that. Suspicious absences, cash payments, dubious connections."

"Maybe he didn't do it for money," Eric suggests. "Which would make it the perfect murder."

Rose furrows her brow. "How so?"

"He means the 'strangers on the train' scenario," I say to her.

The lines on her forehead deepen.

"Two completely unrelated people each need to bump someone off," Flo explains. "They meet on their daily commute, confide in each other, and agree to swap the killings, giving the other guy a chance to have an ironclad alibi."

"How clever!" Rose whips her calendar from her purse and makes a note.

"Come on," Eric says. "There must be *something* suspicious about Quentin. There's something suspicious about everyone."

"Yeah, if you're paranoid," Flo snorts.

"We're amateur detectives," I say in Eric's defense. "If we didn't have a natural inclination for mistrust, we'd see no evil and solve no cases."

"We might even believe Epstein hanged himself," Rose adds.

"Please, stay focused, people!" I turn to Eric. "You're right. We mustn't discard Quentin as a suspect until we've cleared him."

Flo half closes her eyes as if recalling something. "Didn't he go to Dubai after his release from prison? It's a strange choice for a man who lost everything and is starting over as a gardener."

"Landscape designer," I correct her.

"Why is it strange?" Rose asks.

"First, because life there isn't cheap," Flo says. "And second, because the place is in the desert. How many landscape designers do you need to water a dozen palm trees?"

While we're pondering her questions, she adds, "Wouldn't his chances have been better in Normandy, Brittany, or across the Channel, where nature is lush and gardens abound?"

Hmm. "I'm sure Salman will give us a simple explanation for Quentin's choice when I ask him. But your questions are valid, and it would be remiss of us to dismiss them."

Rose flips a strand of silver hair back. "Good detectives, even if they're hobbyists, don't dismiss any questions."

"What about our main suspect, Horace Rapp?" Flo asks. "How do we talk to him?"

We fall silent, thinking. Flo reopens Horace's social media on her phone to search for a clue. The rest of us gaze at the river. A dead branch with a bird perched on it sails past our picnic spot.

Eric sends it the Vulcan "live long and prosper" salute. "My kind of creature! Why exhaust yourself flying when you can ride a drifting twig?"

"In case you were wondering," I say to Rose, "it's about me biking and him driving."

Flo looks up from her screen. "Horace doesn't seem to be a member of any clubs. If he worked out in a gym, he doesn't post about it."

"I could call his office and pretend I want him to install AC in the pâtisserie," I say.

"It's a big company he works for." Flo taps her chin with her finger. "You'll get a secretary who may send you another contractor."

"Have you been able to deduce what Leon does for a living?" I ask her.

She nods. "He's a dog groomer."

"Do you have an address?"

She opens the online Yellow Pages. "Fifteen rue Marie Curie, Pont-de-Pré."

"It's the same village where Coralie lived," I remark. "Maybe he operates out of his house."

"The one he may've inherited from Coralie," Eric says, catching my drift.

"The one that he may be sharing with Horace," Rose offers.

I rub at my ear. "That's unlikely, but you never know."

As if struck by the same idea, all four of us turn to stare at Lady napping at Rose's feet.

I go first. "Doesn't she look like she needs a haircut?"

Flo cups her cheek. "It's urgent."

Lady half opens an eye.

"She had the full works only three weeks ago." Rose swoops Lady into her lap. "If we were professional PIs we'd send the bill to the client."

"It's on me." I grab my phone and look up Leon's number.

"Careful! Some groomers can be pricey," she warns me.

I find the number on Leon's website.

"Last year," I say to Rose, "you witnessed with your own eyes what historical reenactment buffs can spend on their hobby."

"True," she concedes.

I press the Call button. "We're super frugal compared to that."

As we wait for someone to answer, she mutters something under her breath that may or may not be, "Frugal won't get Serge back into my bed."

CHAPTER 7

Four long ringtones later, a man picks up. "Pretty Pooch of Provence Salon, how can I help you?"

"Hello, I'd like to book an appointment." I put him on speakerphone. "How much do you charge?"

"Depends on what you'd like us to do and the breed of the dog."

"She's a Cavalier King Charles spaniel."

I hear the rustle of pages turning. "OK, so, if you go for our full package, then it would be ninety euros."

Gesticulating wildly, Rose whispers, "No way!"

Since I'm paying, I disregard her opinion. But if I go for a cheaper option, I'll be able to return for more later.

"What does your full package involve?" I ask the man, wondering if it's an assistant or Leon himself.

The voice is youthful, suggesting someone in their early twenties. I picture Leon as a thirtysomething, but I may be wrong.

"Shampoo, blow dry, brush out, and a haircut in your desired style," the man replies. "We'll also clean your dog's ears, trim the nails, and brush the teeth."

"Let's do the bath and haircut only," I say. "How much would that be?"

"Seventy euros."

Rose whistles.

"If it sounds expensive," the man says, "remember that those are the most labor-intensive and time-consuming procedures. Besides, my boss is the best dog groomer in the area. He'll never hurt your baby."

Ah, an assistant then. And such endearing loyalty! Makes me wonder if Eric and Flo speak of me as highly as this guy does of Leon.

"When can Lady and I come by?" I ask.

"May 6?"

"That's two weeks from now!"

"We're popular," he says.

I begin to say yes to his proposed date, when he cuts in, "In fact, we just had a cancelation, so if you can swing by within the next hour…"

"How long would the grooming take?"

"If you drop your dog off in the next thirty minutes, we can have her ready by five."

"I can drop you off," Rose offers to me, "but I can't stay or come back for you. I have an appointment this afternoon."

Don't you always?

Long retired, my grandmother lives the life of an active diplomat. Her official duties include Queen of Beldoc, head of a micro party called Environment, Life, Future or ELF for friends, and opposition leader in the municipal council. Those things alone keep her busy enough. But she also runs a book club, teaches doga, and volunteers for a bunch of charities and interest groups.

Nodding to Rose that I don't mind, I say into the phone, "Great. I'll be there."

The assistant takes my name and phone number.

Within minutes we've packed everything away and cleaned up. Rose, Lady, and I jump into her Nissan. After we strap in, we drive off, and Rose opens the roof to give Lady a rush of air that makes her ears flap in the wind. She loves it.

The village of Pont-de-Pré, albeit not as famous as Baux-de-Provence or Gordes, is pretty enough to attract tourists. But I've only ever driven by. One does not *tour* a nearby town. One goes there on business or a family visit or to meet with friends. Given that none of the above ever applied, I managed to reach the ripe age of thirty-two without setting foot in Pont-de-Pré.

When we reach a verdant valley with a medieval bridge that gave its name to the bourg, Rose slows down at the speed limit sign. We drive upward through the narrow streets, turning where the know-it-all GPS orders us to turn.

Eh bah, I must admit that Pont-de-Pré is holding up better than my charming but crummy hometown.

Here, everything is picture-perfect. The limewash is pristine. The uneven houses have been buttressed in a way that takes away none of their authenticity. The cypress-lined streets snake through well-kept façades in hues of ocher. There's no shortage of tiny squares with a tree and a drinking fountain in the middle. Most of the houses in the center have been converted into trendy shops selling souvenirs, wine, and cheese. I spot a boulangerie, a café, a restaurant, and a small art gallery.

Can it belong to Yoona Han, the young artist that Horace Rapp has been buying paintings from?

The bossy GPS guides us to a sprawling house at the edge of the village, bookended by vineyards on one side and woods on the other.

Its midsection looks much older than its east and west wings. Narrow and tall with a sloping roof and small windows, it's a type of smallish traditional Provençal house called *mas*. The uncommon flanks, equipped with bay windows, are much squatter. They make the midriff look like a tower.

The wings are equal in size and shape, but the symmetry stops there. A wooden screened porch runs the length of the east wing. The west wing has a veranda with shutters on the outside and Venetian blinds on the inside to protect the interior from prying eyes. A separate entrance is marked by a sign, Pretty Pooch of Provence.

That's where I head with Lady trotting next to me as Rose drives away.

I press the buzzer, and the gate screeches open. The door to the house, left ajar, chimes softly as Lady and I step in.

The front room sports a counter and shelves lining the wall opposite the entrance. Displayed on the shelves are bags of dog food, leashes, bone-shaped treats, and other dog stuff from a variety of companies. I'm assuming it's all for sale. Next to the counter is a closed door to what must be the grooming area, judging by the barking, whining, and whirring sounds that come from within.

On the other side, a waiting area with chairs and a coffee table is delimited by a row of artificial plants.

"Bonjour," I greet the young man behind the counter. "I'm Julie. We spoke on the phone a half-hour ago."

Lady, who's beginning to suspect foul play, hides behind me.

He points at the dog. "And that would be Lady? Do you mind reassuring her while I get her a treat?"

He darts to a cabinet and returns with two dog biscuits.

I remove Lady's leash and pick her up. Her heart is

racing like crazy against my palm. Being bathed is her least favorite pastime, but what's stressing her out right now is that she's never been here before and doesn't know what to expect.

The assistant feeds her a biscuit. That cheap trick puts her in a more relaxed mood, allowing him to take her from me without much resistance. The promise of the second treat keeps her quiet as he turns toward the interior door, blocking her view of me.

"I'll wash, blow-dry, and brush her down," he says, "and then my boss will give her a haircut. Do you have a preferred style?"

"Same as what she has now."

He gives Lady the second treat and opens the door to the grooming room. "See you at five!" With that he carries her away.

If Lady were a human child, this would be the perfect time to run after them and remind her to never, ever take candy from strangers.

I sidle to the left to be able to peep into the spacious room. A familiar smell wafts out of it. Where have I smelled it before? *I know!* At Rose's, when I arrive just after she's given Lady a bath. It's a blend of dog shampoo and wet wool.

On the right side, there's an area with sinks and counters, displaying a multitude of grooming tools and products. Next to it, are six stacked metal pens. Four canines of various sizes and breeds stare at me from them. Two look bored and the other two, anxious as they wait for their turn at the grooming station.

The latter is located on the left. The floor around it is covered with a thick layer of dog-fur clippings. They form a carpet in a palette of earthy tones ranging from brown to cream.

Behind the counter, a fashionably lanky man in his early thirties says "Hi, there!" to Lady as his assistant transfers her to the large sink.

He's on the short side, but not too short. Pleasant looking but not handsome. His most remarkable feature is being uncommonly blond for southern France. His flaxen strands and neat little beard give him an air of a Viking. An undersized Viking, useless in sword fights but great with the shears.

This must be Leon.

He's finishing up a fluffy Pomeranian. I wonder if he'll come out to the front desk while his assistant is busy shampooing Lady. But it looks like today's clients have all dropped off their dogs. There are four of them in six pens, plus the Pomeranian being groomed, plus Lady being washed. Leon has no reason to go out. Unless I give him one.

Looking around for inspiration, I move farther to the left to be in Leon's line of sight. "Do you sell flea and tick tablets here?"

A box won't ruin me, and Rose often runs out of them, so it's a safe bet.

He looks up from the Pomeranian. "We do! I'll be with you in a moment."

"Thanks!

Hearing my voice, Lady barks and then bays for help. You'd think they're torturing her. Perhaps from her perspective, she's being waterboarded.

Leon sets the Pomeranian back in the pen and exits the grooming room, closing the door behind him. "It's best if Lady can't hear you. Does she normally hate being washed?"

"With all her heart."

He gets a box of flea tablets from a shelf. "I recommend these beef-flavored soft chews."

I pay, racking my brain for something to say that would start a conversation.

Desperate, I go with a banal, "What a charming village Pont-de-Pré is!"

"First visit?"

"Yes. Believe it or not, I live in Beldoc, but I managed to never stop here until today."

He chuckles. "You're forgiven. We get enough visitors, and no one here will complain that we're off the departmental road."

"You cherish your peace and quiet, don't you?"

"Very much."

"I saw many old but well-maintained houses in the center," I say appreciatively. "When were they built?"

"Seventeenth and eighteenth centuries, mostly," he says with pride.

"What about your house? The central part looks old, but the flanks seem modern."

"That's because they are!" He flashes his teeth. "My late aunt had made a deal with my brother and me that she'd build two wings with separate entrances to our specs if we moved in with her."

I give him a round-eyed look. "Sounds like a very advantageous deal."

"Wait until you hear the rest of it." He leans forward over the counter. "No rent, just the utility bills."

"Come on, there had to be a catch!"

"A firm commitment that we'll never put her in a nursing home."

I gape with fake awe. "Was she a saint?"

"We were the apple of her eye." He's still smiling, but there's a tinge of melancholy in his expression. "She wasn't supposed to leave us so soon."

If it turns out Leon had poisoned Coralie, then he's

THE BLOODTHIRSTY BEE

wasting his talent grooming dogs. He should go into politics.

Not presuming I can compete, I feign sympathy. "What happened?"

"She suffered a stroke caused by her chiropractor's mistake." He purses his lips, as if to signal he doesn't want to talk about it. "Anyway, yes, Pont-de-Pré is very pretty."

"You guys are taking great care of it."

"Better than you Beldocians, huh?" He gives me a wink. "Our mayor is a history teacher."

It hits me that I have no idea what Victor Jacquet's original occupation was. "Ours has been mayor forever."

"I heard a retired PE teacher tried to dislodge him during the last election, but she failed."

"That was my grandmother, Rose Tassy."

"Respect!" He tips an imaginary hat off.

I parrot his gesture. "Kudos on being so knowledgeable about my town."

"Beldoc is the place where some of us work, and where we go for a movie or a concert or an art exhibit when we get tired of Arles."

"Speaking of art, I spied a gallery in the village."

He puffs his chest. "You should absolutely drop by. The owner is a gifted painter called Yoona Han, and—" He slaps his forehead. "My bad, she's closed today. She had some business over in Arles."

Interesting. He seems very well informed about Yoona Han's schedule. According to Flo's social media research, it's his brother Horace who was a big fan of the up-and-coming local painter. Maybe so is Leon. He's just not into bragging about it online.

He lifts a forefinger. "Wait! Let me check something."

"Sure."

Leon opens a drawer and rummages through it until he

comes up with a flyer the size of a passport. "You're in luck! Yoona will have a booth at the Beldoc Strawberry Fête next Sunday. You can see her work in your hometown."

"I'll have a stand at the festival, too," I say. "I'm a pastry chef. But I'll find a moment to go take a look."

He hands me the flyer. The paintings featured in it seem nice enough.

"How many do you own?" I ask him.

"Only one… I wish I could afford more." He beams. "But business has been good, so I will soon."

If I wasn't suspecting Leon of auntie-cide, I would've concluded by this point that he's a gregarious, amiable, and likable chap.

"Are you heading back to Beldoc or into the village until the pickup time?" he asks.

I point to the waiting area. "Do you mind if I hang out here? I need to catch up with some reading and emailing that I can do on my phone."

"Please," he says. "Would you like a coffee?"

Well, isn't he just the sweetest guy? "I'm good. But thank you."

"I have to get back to work." He points his chin to the interior door. "Holler if you need anything."

Can I have a full confession, please, written and signed?

CHAPTER 8

After Leon ducks back into the grooming room, I settle into one of the hard chairs and open my email app.

The sun-soaked village outside the door is calling to me. I could buy ice cream and enjoy a leisurely stroll through its streets... But the off chance that Leon's brother Horace would stop by keeps my butt in the uncomfortable seat. I'm aware that Horace's turning up, at this time of day, is improbable. What's probable is that he's in somebody's home or office right now installing an AC unit. Or performing maintenance. Or, he could be in his own office, putting together a quote. Even if he left early, why would he pass through Leon's shop? He'd enter his own wing through his own door.

And yet, bored as I am, I don't budge.

It must be the powerful fear of missing out that keeps me put. I read a theory somewhere that risk aversion is stronger in humans than the promise of gain. Mesdames, Messieurs, Julie Cavallo is living proof of that! Has dating Gabriel changed me? Have I finally grown up? Or is it because I'm still shaken from staring Death in the eye last November?

To be honest, there's another reason for my loitering here. I'm hoping for a snapshot. Whether Coralie's death was natural, accidental or homicidal, I have a better chance of catching a scene from her past here in her house than anywhere else.

I open an email from my bank and begin to read it. Within seconds, the lines quake and the letters become blurred. The familiar crackling noise fills my ears. Suddenly, the faint smell of wet wool is gone, and only the minty air freshener remains.

It's happening now! I'm dropping into a snapshot.

What am I in this one? Something small and hard, sandwiched between warm skin and a layer of fabric. The person I'm flush with leans forward and I realize I'm dangling on a chain.

As in... a pendant? Unfortunately, it would appear so.

My current incarnation provides a rather subpar vantage point, especially compared to a clock on the wall that I was last time. But it gets worse. The stupid chain is too long, meaning I'm located below the neckline of the person's dress. Meaning, I'm blind.

This is hands down the worst position I've found myself in any given snapshot. Even when I was a worm half buried in the ground, I could still see what was going on at my eye level. But now, I'm in the dark. I'm assuming the woman who's wearing me is Coralie, and I'm assuming we're in her house. If it turns out she's home alone and she's not in the habit of talking to herself, then this snapshot takes the Golden Palm of the most useless one I've ever had.

"There's a funny tang to this tea," a deep female voice says.

She's over sixty, I'd say. *She's got to be Coralie!*

THE BLOODTHIRSTY BEE

Who is she talking to? I pray it isn't an imaginary friend.

Someone grunts from a distance as if realizing they'd been spoken to. "Hm?"

Sounds like a man. Or a woman in her nineties.

"What blend is this?" Coralie asks.

Come on, answer her, whoever you are!

"Two words," Leon says. "Absolute sweetheart!"

What?

As reality shifts around me again, I realize that Leon is speaking to me, now, in the material world. A trimmed Lady wags her tail, rushing toward me.

Argh!

I squat and open my arms. "She is a sweetheart, isn't she?"

But inside, I'm so mad at the interruption, that even Lady's joy as she puts her soft paws around my neck and licks my cheek does not comfort me. I hug and pet her, breathing in the smell of dog shampoo and a hint of perfume that Leon must've spritzed behind her ears.

All I needed was another minute!

Even less. A few seconds would've sufficed. To Coralie's second question, the person she was with would've no doubt given a more distinct, likely multisyllabic, answer. If it was Leon, I'd recognize the voice. If it was Horace, whom I've never met, at least I'd know it wasn't Leon.

This is so frustrating I want to cry.

"You hate her haircut?" Leon looks at me, crestfallen.

"Oh no! I love it. I just remembered something that ruined my mood, that's all."

Satisfied with my explanation, he goes to the cash register. I pay. Lady dances around me, impatient to get out. Leon hands me a flyer with the price list of his salon's services, while his assistant vacuums up the floor in the grooming room. They both wish Lady and me the best.

Threatening to come back for the nail trimming, I collar Lady and head out the door.

We stroll through Pont-de-Pré for a while. Lady goes to potty, and I try to get over my *snapshotus interruptus*.

An hour later, Rose calls me to say she's free and swoops in to drive us back to Beldoc. On the way, we rehash what I've learned from Leon and from the snapshot. Essentially, crickets. Well, except for the part with the funny-tasting tea. That bit is very suspicious. It would suggest that I caught the moment Coralie was being poisoned—probably by one or both of her nephews.

For the next three hours, I do the books at the shop and call Eric and Flo to bring them up to speed. Ever positive, Eric insists that, paltry as it may seem, the new knowledge has taken our investigation to the next level.

I call Salman next. He doesn't know about my visions, so I just tell him I went to Pont-de-Pré and had a chat with Leon. And that we have a small lead.

On Wednesday, Eric and I redo the displays. No more bunnies and eggs. The *flavor du jour* is strawberry, and the color palette is fifty shades of pink. This week, we're featuring strawberry macarons, merengues, mille-feuilles, tarts, candies, and chocolates.

Thursday and Friday sail by with nothing to report on.

When Saturday arrives, I need all-hands-on-deck. While Flo works in the front shop, and Rose gives her a hand, Eric and I toil away in the lab. We must get everything ready for the Strawberry Fête tomorrow.

Our stand at the festival will be a gluten-free space, except for slices of a giant strawberry tart baked with wheat flour. The tart is a joint creation of Beldoc's bakers and pastry chefs. We started this morning and will finish tomorrow morning, just in time for the kickoff. Eric and I aren't involved in the production of the pastry bases. We're in charge of the icing. It is also our job to rinse, dry, and hull one hundred kilograms of strawberries. The monster of a tart has half a ton of them.

When the clock strikes eight in the evening, we put up the Closed sign. But we aren't quite calling it a day yet. Eric and I tidy up the kitchen. Flo vacuums and wipes all the surfaces in the front shop. Rose brews coffee and tea.

At a quarter past eight, I open the door to Salman and Quentin.

"Salman has told me about all the cases you guys cracked," Quentin says, when the meet and greet is out of the way. "I'm in awe."

Rose gives him a majestic nod. "You should be."

"Please, have a seat," I say quickly, before she can add that we deserve compensation.

Everyone settles in the bistro corner, and I serve drinks.

Her eyes on Quentin, Flo sets her mug down. "Why did you go to Dubai after they released you from prison? Seems like an expensive choice for a man who lost everything."

Quentin shoots Salman an amused glance. "That's a legit question, actually."

I eyeball him, eager to hear his explanation. I hate loose ends.

Quentin's amusement deepening, he addresses Flo. "One of your hypotheses, I'm sure, is that I was paid to kill Coralie Bray."

"That's right," Flo confirms. "You then served your short prison sentence, collected the payment, enjoyed an emir's lifestyle in Dubai, and returned to France once the money ran out."

Quentin's lips paint a sad smile. "You think three months of opulence is worth spending a year in an overcrowded prison, among wife batterers and child abusers?"

"Just to clarify," Eric jumps in, "we don't actually think it's what happened, but we must consider the possibility."

Quentin nods. "I left the country. I needed to put some distance between myself and the injustice that was done to me. Everything in France reminded me of it."

"Fair enough, but why Dubai?" Flo insists.

"I have a good friend who has a successful business there. He said I could stay at his place for a while, and that he'll help me find a job." He glances at me. "My parents sponsored the trip. They're by no means rich, but my dad had some Airbus shares he could sell."

I lean back, relaxing. "What a sweet gesture!"

Quentin's smile loses its bitter edge. "Do you have any other hypothesis in which I'm the bad guy?"

"We do," I admit. "Or rather, we did. We'd considered the strangers-on-a-train scenario, in which two unrelated individuals hook up and murder each other's target."

Quentin raises his eyebrows. "Fascinating! And? Does it work for me?"

"We couldn't find any recent deaths in your family or entourage."

His eyes sparkle with mirth. "My partner in crime could be a hopeless procrastinator."

Everybody cracks up at the ludicrous statement.

"Have you come up with any other theories, apart from the obvious natural death?" Salman asks me.

"One or both of the Rapp brothers may have poisoned their aunt." I point my chin at Quentin. "It remains to be seen if they'd planned to put the blame on you, or you were just collateral damage."

Quentin twists his mouth in disapproval. "If she'd been poisoned, then, I doubt her nephews had had anything to do with it."

"Why not?" Rose asks. "Don't you find it strange that

they never joined you in pushing for a more thorough toxicological examination?"

Quentin rubs his chin. "I do, but... Coralie loved them to pieces. She wasn't rich. And she'd spent her life's savings extending her house so that her nephews could live there comfortably. Even assuming they're heartless monsters, I don't see why they'd want her dead."

"Me neither," Eric says.

I open my palms. "And that, dear Quentin, is why FERJ is taking your case!"

"Because it's hopeless?"

I shake my head. "Because we want to see you vindicated, and we want to find out what the Rapp brothers' deal is."

"It's very kind of you," he says. "I just... I don't know what your rate is, and I'm on a very tight budget, as you can imagine."

I shoot a warning glance at Rose. To Quentin, I say, "Being unlicensed, we work pro bono. It's our hobby."

"I don't know what to say..." He presses his hands to his heart. "You're much too generous!"

"I agree," Rose mutters at the same time as Eric, Flo, and I assure Quentin that we live to solve unsolvable crimes.

CHAPTER 9

The twelve of us come together at dawn.

Under a vast frame tent erected on *Place de la Mairie*, twelve brave men and women shiver in their starched white or black double-breasted jackets, undeterred by the chill. There's no turning back. We've taken a vow to stick together and support each other throughout our perilous quest.

We are the Fellowship of the Pink.

Crushed by the weight of the responsibility that comes with the strawberry, our shoulders stoop. Our expressions are grave and dignified. We barely talk.

Someone uncaps a thermos of fragrant coffee and sets paper cups on the table. We talk more after that.

On our workstations, we lay out our ingredients, mixtures, pastry shells and utensils. As we get down to work, various protagonists arrive. Town officials, festival employees, musicians, and early guests wander in and out of our tent, watching us work. But we pay them no heed.

At nine, the tart is ready. Mayor Victor Jacquet arrives with his fired-then-rehired deputy, Clothilde Valle, and a few other municipal employees and council members. Rose sashays toward us, gorgeous in her traditional *Arlésienne* costume. As Queen of Beldoc, she just opened the Fête with Victor while we, the worker bees at this end of the square, sweated blood over the strawberry glaze. *Figuratively speaking, of course.*

Victor, Rose, the head of the Strawberry Producers' Association, and we bakers gather around the tart. Cameras click, reporters make notes, the public cheers. The Fellowship disbands. We each go to our stand with a tray of mouthwatering tart slices to sell to festival-goers.

My investigative work may be pro bono, but I bake for money. And there's no such thing as free tart.

By ten, the market is bustling. The sweet aroma of strawberries permeates the air. The cobbled square is lined with stalls overflowing with pretty little baskets. Many of the vendors are local farmers who get a chance today to sell their gourmet strawberries directly to the customer.

Crafts and artisan stands mingle with the produce vendors. Most of the stands tease the visitors' tastebuds with strawberry pastries, ice cream, jams, and candy. A tent in the middle of the square hosts Mayor Jacquet's selection of local artists and their works.

A brass band is playing cheery tunes.

Eric and I don't get any respite until about half past noon. With lunchtime looming, people are drawn to the surrounding eateries and sandwich stands. In a couple of hours, they'll come back en masse for our fare. But until then, we can catch our breath.

I drink some water and dive into my backpack for a banana, when I hear a familiar voice and look up.

At the stand on my left, Flo and Tino are introducing a small group of tourists to the local varieties of strawberries on display.

Tino, who's half-Andalusian, is speaking to most of the group in Spanish.

Flo is educating the rest in French. "Did you know that in France, an average person consumes several kilos of strawberries each year? Most of it is grown in the south."

Her group makes appreciative noises.

"The Carpentras strawberries are the best," Flo continues. "Let us ask a pastry chef which variety she would recommend."

At that Flo and Tino lead their flock straight to me.

I clear my throat. "Um… hello. And welcome!"

They greet Eric and me warmly.

"My personal favorite is the Ciflorette variety," I say. "It's orange-red and egg-shaped, very fragrant and a bit acidic like wild strawberries."

Flo motions to the pastries on my stand. "Just so you know, all of this is scrumptious and gluten-free."

"Except the tart over there," Eric says. "In case you're intolerant."

"Julie's Gluten-Free Delights is the only gluten-free pâtisserie in Beldoc and the surrounding area," Flo tells her tourists. "It's also hands down the best one, traditional bakeries included."

Some of the tourists applaud. I half smile and bow, expecting Flo to mention now that she's my sister and part-time employee. But she doesn't. She goes on heaping praise on my creations and making me feel increasingly uncomfortable.

As her tourists line up to buy something from us, I make big eyes at Flo, mouthing repeatedly that she should tell them. She ignores me. My guilty conscience goes into a full "Smite me, oh Mighty Smiter!" mode.

I raise a hand to draw everybody's attention. "Full

THE BLOODTHIRSTY BEE

disclosure! Your guide is my sister. Her praise isn't entirely objective."

Flo blazes at me with such pique that Tino chokes on a stifled laugh. I understand her resentment. What I just did ruined her marketing effort and undermined her authority. But she'd left me no choice.

Eric points out the free samples. "Now that you know the truth, grab one, and decide for yourselves!"

While the tourists do just that, Flo inquires of them, "Have you ever met anyone more ungrateful than this woman?"

The youngest of her group, a man in his forties, raises a finger. Clearly, he failed to detect the 100 percent rhetorical nature of Flo's question.

"Yes?" Tino acknowledges him. "Please, tell us."

"Once, I let my cousin drive my car over the weekend, while I was away. Full tank, and all. He used the car for his side hustle without telling me, crashed it, and then refused to pay out of his pocket when we learned the insurance wouldn't cover it."

Flo puckers her mouth and looks up, to show that she's weighing the relative gravity of the offenses. "Nah, this is worse."

The moment she and her better half take their group away, the town dignitaries arrive at our stand from the other side of the aisle. This lot consists of Victor with his entourage and Rose with her own suite of courtiers.

Once the mandatory photos are taken, Rose's party carries on to the next stand while Victor's lingers.

I use the opportunity to inquire after his nunnery-dwelling sister, Marlene, and his rebellious nephew, Alex. Marlene had sent my relatives and me some gorgeous hand-painted silk scarves for Christmas as a thank you for helping save her son's life a year ago.

"They're happy," Victor says. "Fully reconciled now."

"Is Alex still living a punk's life?"

He crosses his fingers. "Looks like that phase is over. He's been finding his footing."

After Victor and his crew move on, I leave Eric in charge of the stand and dash to the artists' tent. It's now or never. In an hour, when lunchtime is over, an absent vendor would mean a longer wait time, disgruntled customers, and loss of income.

In the tent, I quickly find Yoona Han's corner. Her paintings stand out. Her colors are bold, and her brushstrokes are fierce. As for her price labels, they are positively wild.

Judging by the visitors' faces when they lean down to read the price label underneath a frame, I'm not the only one to think that.

The funny thing is that Yoona's excess contrasts with the artist herself—a dainty petite woman about my age in an elegant black gown. Her heart-shaped face is makeup free but for some cherry gloss to accentuate her Cupid's bow. Frankly, she doesn't need any more than that. Her foxy obsidian eyes and her jet-black mane do a great job bringing out the porcelain-like smoothness of her skin all on their own.

"Bonjour," I say. "I'm Julie Cavallo, a Beldoc pastry chef from the stand over there." I point in the direction of my ephemeral outlet.

"Pleased to meet you, Julie! I'm Yoona Han, the author of these." She points a graceful hand at her canvasses. "I have a gallery in Pont-de-Pré."

"I know."

She arches an eyebrow. "Oh?"

"I was in Pont-de-Pré on Tuesday, for a grooming appointment, and I saw your gallery. But it was closed."

"Leon is your dog's groomer?" She gives me a brilliant smile.

"It's my grandmother's dog," I clarify. "But yes. And he is a big fan of yours."

A male voice booms from behind me, "Not as big as I am."

I spin around.

A blond man in his late thirties steps closer to Yoona and wraps an arm around her shoulders. "Wouldn't you agree, darling?"

Insecure much?

The man looks disturbingly familiar.

Yoona smiles awkwardly. "Horace, please."

Horace! That's why he seemed familiar. He resembles Leon.

OK, formally speaking, it's Leon who looks like Horace, since Horace is older. The brothers have the same gray eyes and hay-colored hair, the same narrow, fine-featured face. Both are on the wrong side of one point seven meters. Except, where Leon is willowy, Horace is robust, making him appear a little shorter.

Also, where Leon's bearded face brimmed with amiability, Horace's clean-shaven mien is stern.

Oblivious to Yoona's discomfort, he persists, "Am I not a bigger fan of yours, *chérie*, than that cheapskate Leon?"

Ooh, this smacks of sibling rivalry! And jealousy. A motive for murder. What I don't understand is why poison your doting aunt when the rival you want to get rid of is your brother?

Yoona murmurs something in Horace's ear and steps away.

He removes his hand from her shoulder.

God is finally smiling down on our investigation! Here I am, talking to Yoona Han, a person of interest in the Coralie

Bray case, and a moment later, my primary suspect Horace Rapp falls into my lap. And I didn't have to leave my home turf!

I wave at Horace. "Hi, I'm Julie Cavallo, a pastry chef. If you're gluten intolerant or sensitive, you should check out my stand."

"I'm Horace, and I have no issues with gluten, but Yoona does," he replies to my delight. "Do you have a more permanent shop in town?"

"Absolutely! Rue de l'Andouillette, across from Tatiana's Bistro."

"Are you new?" he scratches the back of his head. "I haven't set foot on rue de l'Andouillette in a year."

"It's got to be more than a year. I opened for business two years ago."

Yoona shifts her eyes from Horace to me. "I moved into Pont-de-Pré around the same time, but I've been so busy with the gallery that I haven't properly explored Beldoc and the villages in the area yet."

"You're welcome to check out my pastry shop anytime," I say, meeting her gaze. "Now that you know where it is."

She gives a silvery laugh. "Be careful what you wish for! I might become a regular. I'm not allergic, as such, but I do my best to avoid wheat."

"By 'wheat,' you mean the selectively bred Frankenstein monster that we call wheat these days, right?"

She beams. "You nailed it."

I grin back, mighty pleased with myself for establishing a rapport with a protagonist in the Coralie Bray case.

"Pick any painting." Yoona makes a sweeping gesture to her framed canvasses. "I'll give you a fifty percent discount."

Very smooth! I didn't see that coming.

Yoona is an even better salesperson than Magda. Now that she promised to become a patron of mine, and that we bonded over mutant wheat, how can I pooh-pooh her 50 percent discount offer without coming across as a fraud?

Problem is, even at half off, her paintings still cost an arm and a leg.

I survey them before turning to Horace. "Do you have a favorite?"

"I've already purchased my favorites," he says.

"In plural?"

He rolls his shoulders back. *"Oui, Madame."*

How much does an AC installer make to be able to afford several of these paintings, plus the high-end car that Flo found on his social media?

Yoona smiles a Mona Lisa smile, no doubt to hide how curious she is to see if I can extricate myself from the corner she's pushed me into.

You find this amusing, huh?

Suddenly, a gambit reveals itself to me. "These aren't all of the paintings you have on sale, are they?"

"No," she admits. "There are more in the gallery."

I can see it from the flicker of surrender in her eyes that she knows a checkmate is coming.

Coyly, I say, "I know I'd regret it if I pick one now without seeing your entire collection."

"My offer only applies today," she attempts.

"Too bad for me!" I wave goodbye. "It was a pleasure meeting you."

"The pleasure was mine."

I nod to Horace. "And you. Hope to see you around."

He grunts "likewise" while Yoona presses her palms together and bows gracefully.

Horace never takes his eyes off her.

As I rush back to my stand, a new theory of the crime begins to take shape in my mind.

CHAPTER 10

It's relay time when Eric, who's finished his shift, passes the baton to Flo who's just arrived at the pâtisserie. As soon as there's a gap in the customer influx, I submit my new hypothesis to them.

Flo hums thoughtfully as she ties the emblazoned apron around her waist. "A love triangle, huh?"

"You should've seen the way Horace acted around Yoona," I say. "He was possessive, insecure, smitten."

Eric rounds the counter. "What about the younger brother, Leon? Did he appear smitten, too?"

"He admires her a lot." In my mind's eye, I picture his face when he spoke about her in his salon. "I'll eat my toque if he isn't at least a little bit infatuated."

Flo takes Eric's spot behind the cash register. "Let's recap. Beautiful Yoona moves to Pont-de-Pré about two years ago. The Rapp brothers fall under her spell."

"She flirts with both," Eric picks up. "Horace's uncontrollable jealousy pushes him to plot Leon's murder."

"It's called fratricide," Flo remarks.

Eric gives a small nod. "Horace spikes Leon's tea with a

stroke-inducing drug. Tragically, his aunt sweeps in, picks up the mug, and drinks the tea before Horace can stop her."

"Realizing what he's done, Horace freezes up in shock." Flo mimes the scene, her eyes wide with horror, her arm outstretched gesturing *Stop!* and her mouth screaming a soundless *Nooo!*

"Before the poison has kicked in," Eric carries on, "Coralie heads to Quentin's practice for her chiropractic adjustment."

"*Cherchez la femme*," I conclude. "In this scenario, it wasn't about Coralie's money or her house, which the brothers already lived in, rent free. It was about a woman."

The three of us fall silent, thinking.

Flo turns to me. "In this particular case, jealousy is a more plausible motive than money. And your vision of Coralie drinking poisoned tea doesn't rule out a mix-up."

"Oh, and that could explain why"—I stop to catch my breath, overexcited—"why the brothers weren't interested in screening the body for additional substances. They knew all too well what the ME might find if he looked."

"*He* knew," Flo corrects me. "Horace. Leon was the intended victim."

"That's right," I say.

"My house needs repairs," Eric states out of the blue.

Flo and I stare at him.

"I've now asked three different contractors for a quote," he continues. "But even the lowest one is nowhere near affordable."

I have a feeling he isn't just venting. His comment has something to do with the case.

"I guess I could do some of repairs myself—" he carries on.

"Don't!" Flo and I yell at once.

He startles at our vehemence.

Then something flickers in his eyes. He remembered the toll that a botched renovation had taken on my family.

He puts his hands up. "All right, I won't. Anyway, the reason I brought it up is that Coralie Bray must've forked out two hundred grand, if not more, to triple the size of her house."

Flo narrows her eyes. "How likely is a retired PA to have that kind of savings?"

"It wasn't her savings," I say. "It was her available cash. She had to have more where that came from, because she'd told her nephews they'd never need to pay rent."

Flo turns to me. "Maybe Horace's motive wasn't jealousy, after all. Maybe it wasn't even Horace who poisoned Coralie."

"Then who?" Eric asks. "Leon?"

She nods. "Or both of them... in cahoots."

"Hmm..." I tap the tips of my fingers against my lips. "Do you guys still have the spy equipment you bought off eBay for the Ponsard case?"

"Stakeouts?" Flo rubs her hands together. "Cool! I'll take the femme fatale, Yoona. She's piqued my curiosity."

"Dibs on Horace!" I cry out before Eric has a chance to speak.

"No problem, I'll take Leon," he says.

Flo tucks a rebellious strand into her toque. "What about the aunt, Coralie?"

I goggle at her.

She rolls her eyes at my bewilderment. "No, silly, I'm not suggesting we keep tabs on her grave."

"What are you suggesting then?"

"I'm suggesting we find someone who could shed more light on her and on the relationship she had with her nephews."

An idea pops up in my mind. "Her former colleagues! We could pay a visit to the companies she'd worked for."

Flo chews on her lip. "Under what pretext?"

"We're journalists writing a piece on the pros and cons of chiropractic treatments," I begin, thinking aloud. "Coralie is a known victim, and we're doing a profile piece on her."

"We're trying to see what kind of person she was," Eric picks up, "and why she chose to be treated by a chiropractor rather than a massage therapist."

Flo cocks her head. "What if they demand to see our press cards?"

"We're freelancers." I spread my hands apologetically. "Sorry, no press card."

"We'd be more credible with cards," Flo says.

Before she goes ahead and offers to slap some together for us, I flash my palm. "There are lines we mustn't cross."

My sister frowns, perplexed. "How is showing a fake press card different than pretending to be freelance journalists?"

"That's a great question," I begin, scrambling for a sensible answer, when the entrance door chimes.

A customer! Saved by the gong!

But it isn't a customer.

It's Rose, accompanied by Handlebar Igor.

He greets everyone warmly.

I return his cordiality. "Monsieur Lobov, it's nice of you to stop by!"

"Please, call me Igor, I insist!"

"Are your troubles behind you, Igor?" I ask him.

"That's why we're here," Rose replies in his stead. "Igor's accounts have been unfrozen, since he's squeaky clean and has no ties to any warmongering rulers. But in the meantime, his business tanked."

Flo, Eric, and I offer sympathy.

"And Malvina left me," he says.

We commiserate.

"I'm looking to start a new business in Beldoc or in the area," he says. "I don't wish to move too far away, because I love this corner of Provence, but I can't stay in Eau de Provence, either."

"I left Paris after my divorce," I say. "I know exactly how you feel."

"Do you have an idea for a business?" Flo inquires.

He hesitates before smiling softly into his curled mustache. "I love books. It's been a longtime fantasy of mine to open a bookshop. Maybe my current rough patch is a sign that the time is ripe?"

"It is," Rose proclaims.

Flo's lips quirking, she points her index finger upward. "Did the big boss just call you?"

"He could've as well," Rose says. "I know it in my heart that Igor can turn things around and make lemonade out of all his unsold vodka!"

"She means it figuratively," Igor adds quickly.

Rose levels her gaze with mine. "Do you know if Tatiana has found a buyer for her restaurant?"

Oh my God, of course! "Magda would love to buy half of it to extend her shop. She tried to persuade me to buy the other half, but I have no need or funds for it."

"Who's Magda?" Igor asks.

"Magda Ghali is the owner of Lavender Dream, the shop next to Julie's pâtisserie."

Igor peers at me. "Do you think she'd consider me as a business partner? How would she feel about a bookshop as a neighbor to her Lavender Dream?"

"Better than if you envisaged a stinky fast-food joint, that's for sure!" I take a step toward the exit. "Why don't we ask her?"

Rose, Igor, and I duck out and head straight into Magda's overfull boutique.

We wait until she finishes up with a customer, and then I introduce Igor. I recount how he lost his business because of overzealous bureaucrats and how his relationship didn't survive that spot of trouble.

"I'm looking for a fresh start in Beldoc," Igor sums up.

He then goes on to present his business proposition.

Even before Magda opens her mouth, I know she'll say yes. It's the way she ogles him that gives her away, not to mention her friendliest smile. It's the one she reserves for her best customers and hasn't directed at me even once in two years.

Pushing fifty, Magda is single and, I suspect, unhappily so. Igor is in his mid-fifties, and once again available, a fact that I took care to bring up. Which does make me feel a tad manipulative. *But what the heck!* It was for a good cause. Igor's persona, with his virile, well-waxed and curled mustache, his good manners and debonaire charm, is the most effective argument he could've presented to Magda.

"I love books and booksellers," she says when he's done. "I couldn't dream of a better business mate."

"Does it mean you're in?" he asks, leaning forward.

"Hell, yes! No one wants to take any risks these days. No one is in a growth mindset." She shoots me a withering glance. "I was losing hope."

Igor's shoulders slacken with relief. "Dear Madame Ghali—"

She flaps a hand. "Oh, please! Call me Magda."

"Dear Magda, you have no idea how happy I am to hear that!"

"What do you think of my shop as a neighbor?" she asks him with a coquettish smile. "I hope the perfumes, lavender soaps, and scented candles I sell won't bother you. It's all-natural! I don't deal in synthetic."

I purse my lips. Magda has never asked Eric or me if her perfumes bother us.

"Your shop smells amazing!" Igor snuffles the air. "Well, except for that whiff of cigarette smoke. I bet it was the strung-out customer we crossed who'd brought it in."

Magda's smile slips.

Oblivious to her distress, Igor digs himself in deeper. "Stale cigarette smoke is such an ugly, barbaric intruder in this shop among all the delectable perfumes you sell!"

Magda nods, her olive skin turning a sickly shade of gray beneath her makeup.

By my side, Rose gives a sharp, choppy hack. She's coughing to conceal a laugh, I'm sure of it. When she recovers, she steers the conversation toward administrative practicalities and next steps.

Magda's complexion returns to a healthy color.

She knows that Rose and I know the cigarette smell comes from her clothes and hair, lingering after her coffee and smoke break on the sidewalk outside the shop. Her third or fourth of the day. The proverbial Trojan horse that smuggled the "barbaric intruder" into her fragrant shop is Magda herself.

Does Igor's reaction augur badly for their business partnership? Will he withdraw his proposal if he finds out that Magda is a heavy smoker? Will the drywall separating their shops be sufficient to filter out the smell he dislikes so?

I guess we'll find out.

CHAPTER 11

I must've inherited a masochistic gene because it's the fourth time this week that I either get up or go to bed in the wee hours of the morning. But what choice do I have if I'm to get things done?

The first time I got up for a tart. The second time was for an early-morning stakeout. The third time I did some late-night surveillance. Today, I'll be tailing Horace again, but hopefully with better luck.

On my inaugural stakeout, I trespassed on the Rapp property to get as close to Horace as possible. He went for a jog at dawn. By the time I prowled to the gate, there was no trace of him on any of the three possible directions he could've taken. I picked one and spent thirty minutes trying to catch up with him. My cute sneakers weren't really made for running, getting lost, and then figuring out how to get back to the house. I managed, almost two hours later and soaked in sweat, just in time to watch Horace drive off to work.

I biked home, showered and went to work. In the evening, I said no to an unplanned date night with Gabriel and returned to Horace's garden with a sound amplifier, miserable but proud of my unwavering commitment. Horace's car was parked in one of the sheds, so I figured he'd be at home. My bionic ear picked up nothing, though. Either Horace was so tired he'd gone straight to bed, or he'd headed out on foot, and I'd missed him. After one in the morning, I gave up and went home, cursing the world.

But I learned from that mistake.

This morning, I should be able to shadow Horace on his jog. And in the afternoon, I'll return early enough to spot him leave the property, or perhaps receive a visitor. Unfortunately, I'll have to wait until I have an automobile and a chauffeur—Rose—to tail Horace as he drives around the area installing AC during the day.

I can't wait for self-driving cars to hit the market! Anyone who's been distracted by a vision in the middle of a speedway or who's unfit to drive for whatever reason must feel the same way.

So here I am again, wearing comfortable clothes, proper footwear, and a visor cap. The latter is more for disguise than anything else. A phone strap is wrapped around one of my arms and a black mask around the other. Emergency disguise.

I lurk behind a copse of fragrant bushes in an elevated spot outside Horace's property. The front gate and Horace's screened porch are in my line of sight. I have my binoculars, my phone, and the bionic ear just in case.

It's very quiet at this hour. Most humans and most animals are still asleep. The birds are waking up, but their singing is subdued both in volume and in variety. It's as if they were waiting for the orange ball to reach a point in the sky and give them their cue to blast their full repertoire. The air smells of dewy grass and sweetbriar flowers opening up.

THE BLOODTHIRSTY BEE

I train my binoculars on the house, determined not to miss Horace's exit this time. A mere quarter of an hour later, the entrance to his wing of the house gapes and lets him out. In his jogging outfit, complete with a small backpack and a sweatband, he looks less dapper than during the Strawberry Fête, but more athletic. He opens the screen door to the porch, runs down the steps and crosses the front yard. Stopping at the gate, he does some stretching exercises.

My binoculars never leave him.

As he opens the gate and heads down the road, I scramble behind him. He turns a corner. I resist the urge to accelerate. The trick is to shadow him throughout his morning workout, keeping far enough away to avoid being heard or seen, but close enough not to lose sight of him. Finally, I turn the corner, and exhale with relief. He's jogging along the road. When the road veers left toward the fields, so does he.

After he's been jogging for about ten minutes, he pulls a flask from the bottle pocket of his backpack. He stops for a moment, unscrews the cap, drinks, and sticks the flask back. I use the opportunity to snap a few pics with my phone, just in case.

Horace resumes the jog.

I follow at a safe distance, though I'm beginning to feel a bit tired and slightly short of breath. Suddenly, I realize I can't see Horace anymore. There's too much vegetation and overgrowth along the trail. The fields gave way to a wooded area that obstructs my view.

I sprint for a few minutes, until the trail forks. Which way from here? I can't see very far because of the shrubbery. To make matters worse, a bird launches into a bout of hysterical chirping, which makes it impossible to hear Horace's footfalls or pebbles skittering over the ground.

Which way should I go?

Did he turn left and go downhill to jog along the stream? Or right for some uphill cardio? My rational brain tells me Horace would pick the latter. But the lazy romantic in me favors the more scenic route. Let's face it, I'm not as fit as Horace is, and my body resents the effort required for the uphill trail.

After a moment's hesitation, I let my feet follow the path of least resistance, the one that meanders down to the stream. When I reach the watercourse, and finally get an unobstructed view of the trail, I regret my irrational choice.

I drink some water, take a deep breath, and hightail it back to the more challenging trail.

What a fool I am!

Horace has probably wrapped up and returned to the house already, and by the time I get there, he'll have left just like the first time. While it's possible I would've seen nothing suspicious if I'd tailed Horace properly, by doing it so badly I've made sure I get no results. Yet another morning wasted due to my incompetence!

To think that Rose wanted me to do this for money!

My cheeks burning with shame and my throat on fire with the exertion, I begin to pray that Flo and Eric have better success with their targets later this week. But then, I notice someone about fifty meters ahead on the trail.

It's Horace! I can't see his face, but I recognize his outfit. He isn't running. *What is he doing?*

I grab my binoculars and bring him into focus.

Ha-ha-ha, Horace is being attacked by a bee! Or perhaps it's a wasp. More than one, in fact. Thanks to my sound amplifier, I can hear their angry buzzing. He swats at them and flaps his hands like crazy to brush them off his arms and face.

Pulling my phone from its strap, I click off some

pictures. Horace's fighting off a gang of upset bees is, obviously, of little relevance to the case I'm investigating. But taking pictures of my subject *in action* creates an illusion that something happened during this boring jog. It also allows me to feel like a real gumshoe for one hot second.

Horace curses loudly and stares at his right forearm. I zoom in on it. The area just below the elbow is reddening and swelling by the second. Poor thing, he got stung! Poor bee, too, because once they sting, they die. The critter must've been particularly upset to go the kamikaze route.

Horace rummages in his backpack but doesn't seem to find what he's looking for. Swearing again, he races down the trail, away from the bees.

I duck behind a tree as he zooms past me. Once he's far enough, I return to my initial observation point behind the prickly sweetbriar. My mouth is dry. I have a side stitch, and all my muscles are sore. Rose is right. Bicycling ten minutes to the pâtisserie and then ten minutes back home doesn't count as exercise. I need to find the will and make time in my day for a proper workout.

Plonking myself down I gulp the rest of the water. While drinking, it occurs to me that Horace's panicked flight from the bees may be less comical than it looked. What if he has a history of bad allergic reactions to bee stings? What if it's serious enough to make him rush home to administer himself a shot? Is that why he was rooting through his backpack?

Should I trespass again and eavesdrop to make sure he's all right? *Why am I even hesitating?*

I jump to my feet and trot to the fence that delimits the property. Last time I had to climb over it because the gate was latched. Good thing I'm a better climber than runner! But this time the gate is open, so I just walk in.

Before I reach the house, an ear-piercing wail makes me jump. An ambulance pulls up at the gate and maneuvers into the front yard. I dash for cover behind a tree. The door to Horace's quarters swings open. He staggers out on the porch, all red and swollen. As the paramedics scurry toward him with a gurney, Leon's door opens. He runs out, takes in the scene, and rushes to his brother.

Horace collapses. I hear him thrash and struggle for breath, but the full panels that replace the railing on his porch hide him from view. The paramedics hunker down around him and do their thing, exchanging brief comments. Their alarmed voices suggest it isn't looking good.

What's going on? Did he stop breathing? Are they giving him CPR? Oxygen? I wait for long minutes, biting my nails, until the white coats dash down the porch and back to the ambulance, with Horace on their gurney.

He isn't suffocating or writhing anymore. In fact, he doesn't move at all.

CHAPTER 12

I'm not sure how I got back to my apartment.

I mean, it's clear that I bicycled, but I have zero recollection of what I saw or heard on the way. It's a miracle I didn't get hit by a commuter speeding to get to work on time or flattened by a distracted trucker. It was pure luck that the drivers that traveled the same roads as me in the direction of Beldoc were all awake enough for both themselves and me.

Horace hadn't been so lucky this morning.

As soon as I'm in through the door, I grab my phone and dial Gabriel.

Pick up, pick up, pick up!

"Julie?" His voice is hushed. "Can I call you back?"

"It's kind of urgent."

"Are you in danger?" he whispers.

"No."

"Is it Rose, or Flo, or Eric? Is Lady in danger?"

"No, but—"

"I'll call you back in an hour," he says, cutting me off. "I really can't talk now." He hangs up.

What now? Do I go to the gendarmerie and recount that I saw Horace jogging and getting stung by a bloodthirsty bee? Or should I first tell Gabriel and see what he advises me to do? If the cops make me testify under oath, I'll have to reveal I was spying on Horace as part of an unsanctioned investigation into his aunt's death.

Alternatively, I could give the police the information with an anonymous call.

My feverish mind immediately enacts the conversation.

Me: "Hello, this is Mystery Eyewitness."

Desk officer: "Could you spell that for me, please?"

Me: "Er... What I mean is I'm calling anonymously from an undisclosed location."

Desk Officer: "Ah, all right then. What do you wish to report, Madame?"

Me: "I was lurking around Pont-de-Pré at dawn, as is my habit, when I saw a bee sting Monsieur Horace Rapp."

Desk Officer: "By Jove! There are no words to express how grateful we are for this hot tip, dear Madame!"

Me: "Wait, I'm not done. He had a severe reaction to the sting."

Desk Officer: "Did you call for help?"

Me: "He did."

Desk Officer: "Did help arrive?"

Me: "It did."

Desk Officer: "Wonderful. Anything else?"

Me: "Nope, I have nothing else to say. Absolutely nothing at all. I'll just go back to my law-abiding life then."

Desk Officer: "Before you do, may I ask you something?"

Me: "Go ahead."

Desk Officer: "Madame Julie Cavallo, pastry shop owner, calling from Beldoc—"

Me: "Wait, I never gave you those details!"

Desk Officer: "But your phone did. Tell me, why were you

snooping around Monsieur Horace Rapp's house, Madame Cavallo?"

Me: "This is a mistake. I don't know any Julie Cavallos from Beldoc. I'm just a random vigilante from Belgium. Oh, and I'm driving into a tunnel. Can you hear me? I can't hear you. Beep... Beep... Beep."

Lame, I know.

My dilemma isn't as simple as it may appear. If Horace survives the attack, which I sincerely hope he does, then my testimony will be perfectly useless. Even in the unfortunate event that he dies, will the authorities really need my intel to figure out what happened? I bet he'd mentioned the bees to the paramedics when he called 112. And if he hadn't, then the medical examiner should be able to tell what killed him.

I pace my tiny apartment for a while, as I decide on the best course of action. Seeing as there's nothing I can do to help Horace at this point, I may as well stick to the original plan, which is to wash, change into clean clothes and head to the pâtisserie.

And that is exactly what I do, suddenly finding immense comfort in my daily routine.

∼

GABRIEL, Eric, and I are standing in a tight circle by the counter, our heads down and our jaws set. Eric has locked up the entrance door and flipped the sign. I've removed my chef's hat and raked my hands through my hair with such ferocity it's now fanning out around my face in a crazy-professor style. But I don't care. Anything that can help me drain some of this nervous energy, I'll take it.

I look up at Gabriel. "Is he completely, irrevocably dead?"

He gives me *the look.*

"I mean, dead bodies do wake up sometimes, you know?" I massage my scalp again. "It's a well-documented phenomenon. The heart can restart spontaneously after it's stopped beating for a while."

"Horace Rapp was pronounced dead by a bunch of medical professionals two hours ago," Gabriel says. "The chance that he'll wake up is one in a trillion."

It's a done deal then. My prime suspect just died on me.

I feel sorry for him. The other person I feel sorry for is Leon. While I did suspect Horace of trying to poison Leon, I never regarded Leon as the bad guy. He seems like a genuinely nice person. He loves dogs. He loved his late aunt, Coralie. I'm sure that despite competing with Horace for Yoona's heart, he loved his brother, too. And now, he'll be all alone in that ungainly house big enough for all of them.

Eric was supposed to tail him all day tomorrow while I kept the fort, but that plan now seems inappropriate.

I glance at Eric and then at Gabriel. The latter phoned me back an hour after my panicked call like he'd promised. I'd just arrived at the shop. I gave him the lowdown and asked him to find out if Horace had made it. Another hour later, Gabriel walked into the pâtisserie, waited until there were no customers, and delivered the bad news.

I swallow hard, wringing my hands.

He takes them into his. "Julie, there's no reason to panic. But I do recommend you come with me to the gendarmerie and give a written statement."

"Is she in trouble?" Eric asks him, a deep crease forming between his eyebrows. "Will she be treated as a suspect?"

"Absolutely not! Her spying and trespassing didn't cause Horace Rapp's death. Once the autopsy is done, the ME's report will corroborate her account."

Eric's brow smooths. "Phew."

"That being said, she'll have to explain why she was

tailing Horace Rapp." Gabriel releases my hands and glowers at me. "Against my advice."

I lift my eyes upward. "Poor Quentin!"

"Quentin?" Eric and Gabriel ask at the same time.

"My testimony may entail more unpleasantness for him," I say. "It's vital that I impress upon the gendarmes that reopening the Coralie Bray case and tailing Horace were my initiative. Not his."

"With some luck, the officer interviewing you will be Sophia," Gabriel says.

"Sophia Firmin?" I ask, barely containing my joy. "Vero's best friend?"

Not only is Lieutenant Sophia Firmin my older sister's bestie, but she's also someone I had a chance to help last spring.

At last, Fate is cutting me some slack in this messy, hopeless case! If any officer of the law can be expected to show benevolence toward me, it's Sophia. Not Gabriel, who's always been as preachy as helpful.

"Pont-de-Pré is within her brigade's jurisdiction," Gabriel informs me before curling his lip. "I wish it were within Beldoc's! I'd make sure we assigned the task of interviewing you to the most curmudgeonly, most ill-tempered officer."

I scowl. "Of course, you would."

"But don't worry," he says, the threat in his tone contradicting his words, "I'm going to ask Sophia to give you a really hard time. Because you deserve it."

"Pff!"

He cocks his head as if suddenly recalling something. "You mentioned you took pictures this morning. Show me."

I get my phone.

The three of us start by looking at the first series of unfathomably mundane pics I took when Horace stopped to drink some water. There are dozens of them. If you put them back-to-back, you could make a movie.

Why didn't I toggle to video? No doubt because, in my head, I had the image of the private detective zooming and clicking off picture after picture, all of which she would then print for the client to justify her fee.

"Great job, Chef," Eric cheers.

His expression is deadpan, making it hard to tell if he's being sincere or sarcastic. From the corner of my eye, I notice Gabriel's mouth twitch.

We move on to the second series, the one with the bee attack, and suddenly, no one is smiling. Under different circumstances, we would be entertained, watching Horace's clumsy attempts to get rid of his minuscule assailants. But the knowledge of what happened gives a tragic tang to every frame.

"Hold on!" Gabriel stops my swiping fingers. "Go back."

I swipe to the previous photo.

He points at one of the trees in the background. "Zoom in here."

Dutifully, I do.

And then my jaw drops.

Next to me, Eric cries out, "What the hell!"

There's a man behind the thick tree trunk. Only a third of him is visible, but it tells us plenty. He's on the shorter side, thin, straight blond hair. His face is concealed by a mask and big dark sunglasses. In his hands, he's holding a birdhouse.

Oh. My. God. It isn't a birdhouse. It's a small beehive.

CHAPTER 13

Here I am again, between the gray walls of the austere interview room of the Beldoc Gendarmerie. I glance at Sophia sitting across the table from me. She's kept a professional distance, but her gaze is warm when it meets mine. By contrast, there's no emotion whatsoever in the piercing eyes of hierarchical superior, Capitaine Loubardin.

Sophia and Loubardin came down from Bellegarde this morning to take my statement.

Given the far-reaching implications of the photos I took at the crime scene, it's Loubardin, and not Sophia, who's conducting the interview. Sophia intervenes every now and then to ask for clarification or make a reassuring comment. For all I know, they're playing the good cop, bad cop trick on me.

We're at the point in the interview where I've brought them up to speed and been chastised for doing unsanctioned detective work. I haven't yet given up hope they'll thank me for having photographed the murderer, but I'm not holding my breath.

"Now you know everything I know," I say, looking from Loubardin to Sophia. "Will you share what you know in return?"

Loubardin bursts out in laughter, and then, with a disconcerting lack of transition, he switches back to his poker face.

"We're under no obligation to do that," Sophia says softly.

"But you want me to keep cooperating, don't you?" I infuse my voice with similar softness. "You know, in case I suss out something new."

"This is an active investigation now, Madame Cavallo," Loubardin barks. "You are to stop interfering. And you must tell no one about the photographs you took. We saved them on our computers and removed them from your phone."

"You can't do that! Aren't they protected by copyright or something?"

He crosses his arms. "Would you like to be charged with trespassing on the Rapps' private property, Madame Cavallo? I can certainly arrange that."

Ungrateful bastard!

While I glare daggers at him, Sophia leans forward. "It's evidence, Julie. You must understand that we'd like to keep it close to our chest."

"But Eric and Gabriel—" I stop to correct myself, "I mean, Capitaine Adinian, they saw them already."

"Sophia will call your sous chef after we're done and request his silence," Loubardin says.

"But why? It's not like you can keep Horace's death a secret."

"No, but we intend to keep his suspected murder a secret for as long as possible," Sophia explains.

"Aah, I see."

And I do, as it happens. A famous missing wife case comes to mind. It was in the news for months on end. We learned later that the investigators had sat on some clues pointing to the husband. They'd pretended to believe his tearful show of innocence and grief until they got him to incriminate himself.

I stare Loubardin in the eye. "You believe you can corner Leon Rapp by revealing those photos at the right moment."

The look that flashes across his face before he recovers his neutral expression tells me all I need to know. He suspects Leon of using bees to murder his brother, Horace. Given how much the man with the beehive resembles Leon, that theory makes a lot of sense.

Have they formally charged him yet, I wonder? If my photos are all they've got, then maybe not. In all of them, the killer's face is hidden behind the mask and sunglasses. I'm assuming the gendarmes need to buy time to look for more evidence without spooking Leon.

Loubardin unfolds his arms. "It warms my heart that you understand the importance of trusting the professionals to do their job, Madame Cavallo."

I give him a lackluster nod. "Can you at least tell me what the ME's report says?"

"Sure," he surprises me by consenting. "The autopsy showed two stings, one on the forearm and the other on the neck. One dead honeybee was found on the body. The internal examination revealed pulmonary edema and laryngeal swelling—"

I glance at Sophia for help.

"Swelling of the throat and tongue," she translates.

"The cause of death was concluded to be rebound anaphylactic shock induced by two bee stings."

I scrunch up my face. "Rebound?"

"Rebound anaphylaxis," Sophia explains, "is when the

most severe symptoms occur sometime after the initial allergic reaction without any additional exposure to the allergen."

"Is it common?"

"Rebound or biphasic response occurs in 5 to 20 percent of severe allergic reactions," Loubardin informs me. "It can happen anytime within seventy-two hours of the trigger event."

I close my eyes, replaying the sequence in my head. Horace got stung by the first bee. His forearm reddened and swelled. He rummaged through his backpack, gave up, and sprinted home. He must've been stung again before he managed to get away from his assailants. Once at home, he was able to call an ambulance and give them his address. The choking didn't begin until the ambulance—and I—got there.

"What do you think Horace was looking for in his backpack before he took off?" I ask Sophia and Loubardin. "His phone? An EpiPen?"

"Both," Sophia says.

"Had he left them behind? Did you find them? Where? Had he called the ambulance from his cell phone or his landline?"

Shifting my gaze from Sophia to Loubardin, I continue to bombard them with questions. "Had he been able to use his EpiPen? Did you find it? Was it empty or full? Had he injected himself correctly? Had he said anything to that effect when he called 112?"

Loubardin hastens to reply before Sophia can say anything, "Those are all good questions, Madame Cavallo. Unfortunately, I am not at liberty to answer them."

I blow out a frustrated breath. "What happened to solidarity and cooperation between detectives?"

"You are not a detective," he points out. "You're a baker."

"Pastry chef, if you wish to be specific," I say.

It's like arguing with Gabriel before he gives up on talking sense into me.

I decide to try a different approach, making statements instead of asking questions. "The fact that Horace experienced rebound... erm..."

"Anaphylaxis," Sophia prompts.

"Anaphylaxis," I repeat. "That fact tells me he hadn't found his EpiPen, or he found it empty, or perhaps he screwed up his shot."

A wall of silence is all I get in response.

Not cool, officers! Not cool. I'll obtain the answers to all those questions sooner or later. They could've saved me and our investigation some precious time by providing them now.

Loubardin wraps up the interview shortly thereafter.

We exchange civilities and then I make tracks. While I bicycle back to the pâtisserie, I devise ways for Eric and me to keep the other half of FERJ in the dark. Hiding things from my perceptive and very well-informed grandmother is going to be hard. And it isn't something I relish. Having to lie to my sister while counting on her help with the case is making me feel like crap.

I turn onto rue de l'Andouillette and halt in front of my shop. When I walk in, I find Flo, Rose and Eric there. I glance at Eric who's serving a customer.

"They'll explain," he says to me before turning back to the customer.

Flo motions Rose and me into the lab.

Intrigued, I follow them. "What's going on?"

"I was in Yoona's gallery earlier this afternoon," Flo begins, "trying to decide if she's a comet or a rising star."

"Also, working the case," Rose cues her.

"That goes without saying!" Flo flips her hair back

exactly the way Rose does it. "I was mentally preparing to ask Yoona a question. But then her phone rang. It was Leon."

I raise my eyebrows. "You were able to hear him?"

"No, Yoona said, 'Hi, Leon'."

"Oh."

She continues, "He said something, and she rushed out the door."

"Your sister followed her!" Rose interjects, bursting with pride.

Flo looks left and right, and tiptoes to the right, and then back to the left, while humming "The Pink Panther Theme."

Rose claps her hands.

"Yoona went around the advertising panel outside her gallery for privacy," Flo says. "I stood on the other side of the panel and eavesdropped on her conversation."

Rose beams at me. "Your little sister used the urban landscape to her advantage. Isn't that genius?"

Rose looks at me the way she did when Flo was a toddler and managed to stand up on her own, speak her first word, or make her first drawing. To our grandmother, but also to our dad and to our oldest sister Vero, Flo will forever be the family's baby. The one who lost her mom much too young. The one they did their best to raise to be a happy human being, not someone with a huge, immovable chip on her shoulder.

I give Flo a thumbs-up. "Were you able to overhear anything of interest, genius?"

"Drum roll, please..." Flo pauses for excruciatingly long seconds. "Leon told her Horace was dead. He also told her gendarmes were searching the house."

"You mean, Horace's wing?" I ask.

"Nah, all of it, including Leon's wing." She makes another dramatic pause. "They found Horace's EpiPen!"

"Where?"

"In Leon's quarters!"

I squint at her. "Did he tell Yoona as much?"

"No, but while they were talking, he started yelling at the gendarmes that he had no idea how Horace's EpiPen had put itself into his trash."

"Do you think Leon stole it from Horace's backpack just before the jog?" I ask Flo and Rose.

"It sure looks like it," Rose says. "He stole the pen and then drove, or perhaps rode a bike, to the nearest beekeeper, and he stole the hive."

"Basically, Leon made sure he had the poison, while Horace didn't have the antidote," I conclude.

"All he had to do after that," Flo says, "was lay in ambush in a spot he knew was on Horace's jogging route. The moment Horace turned up, Leon disrupted the hive and let the angry bees do his dirty work."

Rose's eyebrows shoot up and hold. "What a wonderfully diabolical plan, isn't it?"

"Hang on a sec," I say. "Wouldn't the bees have attacked Leon, too?"

Flo shrugs. "So what if they did? First, he isn't allergic. Second, he may have been wearing some strong repellent."

"Peppermint essential oil is great for that," Rose interjects helpfully. "Rosemary and eucalyptus, too."

"Why didn't Horace wear any repellent then?" I ask.

"Because there are no beehives in that area," Flo says. "And bees aren't known to be early risers. They stay put until it's sunny and warm."

"Horace had no reasonable cause to take any special precaution for his jog," I sum up.

"And, in case of emergency, he knew he had his EpiPen," Flo adds.

"Did you learn anything else from Leon's call to Yoona?" I ask her.

She shakes her head. "Only that once the cops found the EpiPen, they asked Leon to end the call and to follow them to the gendarmerie."

"They'll charge him with murder," I say.

Flo counts on her fingers. "One, as a close family member, he knew how bad Horace's allergy was. Two, the EpiPen was in his trash. Three, considering the pictures you took, I'd say Leon did it."

I blink, surprised. "You know about the pictures?"

"Eric told her," Rose says, "and she told me just before Sophia called with the gag order."

Yay! What a relief that I won't have to keep such a crucial detail from half of my team!

Flo eyeballs me. "What was Leon's motive in your opinion? Money? Yoona? Both?"

"We'll find out," I say. "As long as we don't lose sight of our main goal."

Flo knits her eyebrows. "Which is…?"

"Proving Quentin's innocence, of course!" I send her a *d'oh* look. "His fate matters to the Establishment as little now as it did a year ago."

Rose nods. "They won't recognize they'd screwed up unless they're forced to. He won't get justice without our help."

The spark in Flo's eyes tells me she agrees.

CHAPTER 14

⌘

May 1 represents one thing in France, and two things in Bouches-du-Rhône.

In all of France, it's a national holiday called May Day, aka International Workers' Day, aka Fête of the Lily of the Valley.

In the Bouches-du-Rhône department, May Day is also when we celebrate *les gardians*, the herdsmen that look after the black bulls and other cattle that the wetlands of la Camargue are famous for. In Arles, there's a dedicated procession honoring them and their confederacy. Here in Beldoc, a squad of *gardians* has simply joined the main rally, decked out in their traditional dress and mounted on their signature white horses.

All shops and businesses are closed. The weather is perfect. Everyone is out on the streets, either buying a lily of the valley sprig, selling lily of the valley sprigs, or marching among the protestors and waving a lily of the valley sprig.

After a late start, Gabriel and I are finally out. But we haven't joined the demonstration yet. We're hunting for the bell-shaped flower first to protest for workers' rights in good form. Gabriel is hoping to locate a vendor from the trade union of the Gendarmerie Nationale to buy his sprig from. I'm OK with buying mine from the first guy or gal we stumble on even if they can't bake.

The first vendor we cross is a gangly fellow of no more than eighteen.

"Do you have a license?" Gabriel asks him.

You've got to be kidding me!

I pinch his side, hard. "Can't you take a break from policing on your day off?"

The kid's eyes become shifty. "A license isn't required today, is it?"

"Correct," Gabriel admits. "May Day is the only day anyone can sell lily of the valley. No license required."

The kid's face expands into a toothy smile. "Phew."

As if to apologize for his cruel joke, Gabriel buys not a sprig, but a bouquet for each of us, and leaves a tip.

We follow the noise toward the rally. When we reach the procession perambulating down the main street, I'm surprised to see it's much bigger than last year.

How come?

Everyone and their trade union rep are here, helpfully identifying themselves by means of banners held high. Communists, socialists, radical Left, radical Right, liberals, conservatives, Royalists... Clearly, every political formation with the slightest presence in Beldoc or the surrounding villages has showed up. They march waving lily of the valley sprigs, flags, and political slogans.

Horace Rapp's name keeps popping up in a number of slogans, and I realize why May Day has attracted more protesters than usual this year. What with Horace's death covered by both *Beldoc Live* and *Beldoc Soir,* and also the regional press, this year's Labor Day doubles as a solemn march in his honor.

I spot our mayor, Victor Jacquet. His Red-turned-Green Radical Environmentalist Party is leading the procession with enough demonstrators to form three rows. It's easy for him to mobilize so many people, since half of them are employees at the town hall!

Marching in the middle of the front row are the standard-bearers, Victor and Clothilde. Last year, Clothilde left her post as Victor's deputy and resigned from his party to run Rose's campaign for mayor. After Victor won, he offered Clothilde her old job. And she took it.

The Green Radicals' banner reads:

R.I.P. Horace Rapp! Climate Change Kills!
Demand Action from the Government!

Gabriel and I exchange an amused look.

"Do you happen to know what climate change has to do with anaphylaxis?" he asks me.

I didn't until this very moment, as my mind immediately cooks up a hypothesis. "Climate change makes humans prone to allergies."

He appears in doubt. "Does it?"

"I have no clue," I confess. "But I have more ideas! Climate change makes bees angrier. Confrontational bees become ferocious. Unstable bees go berserk. Bee venom becomes radioactive."

"Hmm."

"Oh, oh, here's a good one!" I shoot him a triumphant look. "Climate change kills bees, which causes honey to become so scarce that people suffer a heart attack when they see the price of a jar."

He looks me up and down. "I understand now why you do what you do. All that wild imagination needs an outlet."

"What? Not one of my theories is good enough for Monsieur Professional Detective? Let's hear yours then!"

"Look, look, that's Rose over there," he deflects, pointing into the crowd.

There she is, indeed. And not alone.

My grandmother's Green Conservative Micro party is represented by her usual cronies, including Marie-Jo Barral, the editor in chief of *Beldoc Live*, and Sarah Owen, Rose's bosom friend. Rose and Sarah have brought along their canine babies, Lady and Baxter, tucked safely in doggie carriers. I spot Igor, too, his mustache curled even more than usual for May Day. And, marching with them, is a person who until now never hesitated to voice her contempt for the spoiled workers and their too-generous rights—Magda Ghali.

The banner that the Green Conservatives brandish, announces:

R.I.P. Horace Rapp! Government Overreach Kills!
Respond With Civil Disobedience!

I glance at Gabriel. "You have three minutes to deduce the reasoning behind this one."

"Your grandmother has even more imagination than you do," he replies. "And her mind works in truly mysterious ways."

You don't know half of it.

"Her ways aren't mysterious," I say. "They are certifiably unknowable."

Gabriel and I fall in stride with the protesters, but stay on the sidewalk, since there are no openings anywhere in the central strip. When the crowd reaches the corner to head down to the riverfront, it shifts, bringing Victor's and Rose's gangs closer together. Too close for their comfort.

"Climate deniers!" Victor shouts at Rose and her friends.

"Fearmongers!" she yells back at Victor's crew.

One of Victor's staffers parries, "Hippie anarchists!"

"Closet Stalinists!" Sarah rebuffs.

Rose and her team cheer.

Clothilde shakes her fist and hits them with, "Cynolatrists!"

Everybody reaches for their smartphones to look up the word.

"It means *dog idolizer*," Gabriel informs me looking up from his screen.

We watch Rose stick her phone back in the pocket of her jeans as her face blanches and her jaw tightens.

"Rose was going to forgive Clothilde for returning to Victor's employ," I say to Gabriel. "But she won't let this one slide."

He skews a crooked smile. "What level of retaliation do you predict on a scale from 'How could you?' to 'Burn in hell, you, backstabbing Judas'?"

"Hard to tell…"

Rose opens her mouth to respond to Clothilde, but Magda shoves an elbow into my grandmother's side. "Don't!"

Rose turns to her. "Why not? She just went for the jugular."

Magda whispers something in Rose's ear, pointing her chin at Igor.

Fuming, Rose shuts her mouth.

I explain to the incredulous Gabriel that Magda must've reminded Rose that they're going to need Victor if their project is to succeed. It's in his purview to authorize or not the repurposing of Tatiana's restaurant for retail and the splitting of the space into two separately-owned shops.

"Rose, as opposition leader in the municipal council,

always makes sure to give Victor a hard time," I add. "And now, after this public bickering…"

"It's probably kaput for Magda and Igor," Gabriel fills in.

We walk in silence for a while, until Gabriel speaks, "You should be feeling very pleased with yourself, *non?*"

"Should I?"

He ganders at me. "You provided officers of the law with evidence and an eyewitness account that helped them charge Leon Rapp with murder."

"They found Horace's EpiPen in Leon's trash."

"True, but thanks to you, their case is much stronger."

Why is he suddenly so supportive of my detective work?

He searches my face. "You'll let Capitaine Loubardin do his work now, won't you?"

Ah, I see why.

"Do you expect him to reopen the Coralie Bray's case?" I ask. "Do you think he'll believe Quentin now?"

From Gabriel's uncomfortable silence, I can tell he doubts it.

"Besides…" I pause, looking for the words to convey the unease I've felt since the news of Leon's arrest. "There are things about Horace's murder that don't add up."

"Like what?"

"Like why on earth would Leon toss the EpiPen in his own trash can?"

Gabriel waves dismissively. "He had no time to dispose of it properly, because he had to dash out for the beehive. I'm sure he meant to get rid of the garbage after the deed was done."

"Yet he didn't."

"Because he didn't expect Horace's symptoms to be delayed, which allowed him to get back home and call 112."

"Still…" I click my tongue on the roof of my mouth,

thinking. "The gendarmes' hypothesis is that Leon had planned for the murder to look like accidental death, right?"

"That's right."

"Well, then his plan was too dumb to be true."

"How do you mean?"

"It was overelaborate," I say. "And, at the same time, sloppy."

"Because of the EpiPen in the trash?"

"Not only." Halting, I turn to face Gabriel. "He took care to hide his face but he couldn't be bothered to wear a cap? Blond hair like that is uncommon in our parts."

He considers the point I made. "Maybe Leon simply forgot the cap... or lost it."

"Don't you find that a little too careless for someone committing premeditated murder?"

"I do," he admits. "How would *you* have gone about it?"

"About what? Murdering my last surviving family member?"

"Yes."

"Off the top of my head..." I scratch said top, scrambling for a foolproof plan.

"I'm waiting, Madame Cavallo."

"It's not that I lack ideas," I say. "It's more that they involve purchasing some sort of poison or using a murder weapon that could be traced back to me."

"See? Homicide isn't as easy as it seems."

"Thank you for crushing my illusions!" I pout, annoyed. "Looks like I'm no criminal mastermind, after all."

He laughs. "Neither is Leon. He's a dog groomer who went rogue and decided he could get away with murder."

It's hard to argue with that, so I don't.

We follow the rally from the sidelines, until it gets to its stationary phase, and the trade unionists launch into interminable speeches. At that point we decide we can do something more fun back at my place.

On paper, Gabriel has given me a perfectly sensible explanation for Leon's cavalier approach to murder. A more experienced criminal, or someone more knowledgeable, would've done it in a way that was both simpler and more effective. But Leon is no contract killer. He's a guy with a motive who found a clever means in the bees and a great opportunity in the jog. And then he made a muck of it.

People often do.

CHAPTER 15

Tonight, we're catering a party for one of our local nabobs, Jean-Louis Ponsard.

Some fifty guests have gathered at his villa in the gated community near the marina. To my great relief, Denis isn't here for once. I believe he's across the Channel for business these days.

I've rounded up both Eric, Flo and Tino, Flo's boyfriend, to slave away with me tonight. It's good money, so no one's complaining.

Ever since FERJ helped solve the murder of his mother-in-law, Jean-Louis and his wife Valerie have never entertained guests, be it business or private, without me baking for them. What happens is they order a selection of our pastries, which Eric and I deliver. The serving has always been done by the crew of their go-to chef, who also puts together the rest of the menu.

But tonight, Beldoc's most glamorous fortysomething couple is having a special event—a *vin doux* tasting.

The domain they'd purchased and heavily invested in not so long ago has now produced its first vintage of organic, biodynamic *muscat blanc à petit grains*. The Ponsards' muscatel is on the sweeter side, a proper full-bodied and fruity dessert wine. Ergo, cheese and zesty pastries are a better choice to accompany it than savory dishes, which pair well with drier muscatel.

Ergo, Julie Cavallo is in charge of the catering from A to Z!

Tino is manning the cake and coffee bar, and the rest of us slalom among the guests with our trays loaded, our postures upright, our buttoned-up uniforms spotless, and our smiles charming without being flirty. That's what we aim for, anyway. We serve wine and pastries, bus tables, and engage in friendly but brief conversations when spoken to. In addition, I multitask, keeping a watchful eye on everything as a chef should.

This isn't a seated dinner, but it's no paper cups and petit fours party, either.

The Ponsards always receive in style, with crystal and china, and starched linens. The cutlery is no silver-looking plasticware. It's real silver. All the above, except for the linens, is supplied by the hosts. Normally, I avoid relying on the house for supplies or equipment when I cater. But if the host insists on silver, it's either use theirs or borrow Rose's heirloom collection, which she'd never let me do. So, there you go.

My mind takes note of the little details, a raised hand or expectant look, a spot to clean, a question to answer. The guests are having a good time, relaxed and chatty in their wine-and-sugar-induced euphoria. *Good.* That's exactly how I want them to be.

Every now and then, I dart to the kitchen for more cheese or pastries, or to send Eric to the cellar for more wine. It's important to keep the flow uninterrupted.

I'm cruising with a loaded tray when I notice an

THE BLOODTHIRSTY BEE

animated group with several glasses that are empty. I beeline to them. Most opt for more muscatel.

A woman hands over her wine glass. "May I have some water, please."

"Evian, Perrier, or homemade infused water?" I ask in the professionally amiable tone I picked up during my years in Paris.

She points out the infused water. "That one would be lovely."

"Excellent choice," I compliment her.

Spruced up with strawberry slices and mint leaves, this is my single highest-margin fare, across all categories. Cheap and easy to produce and replenish, a popular win-win.

I'm heading back to refill my tray when I spy an unusually tall man in his late forties. He's standing near the doorway, talking with another guest. He looks familiar, even though I don't think I've met him before. At least, not in real life—

A mental image makes me stop in my tracks. I've seen this man before, in a snapshot I experienced by the fateful beach house. He was younger and thinner in that vision. He didn't have a beard. Also, his eyes are brown, while they were blue in the vision. But the shape is the same. And, just like in my snapshot, there's something off with them.

Is he wearing color lenses?

And that expression... and the way he carries himself... What if it's really him? What if it's the negligent contractor whose shoddy work caused that newly renovated house to explode and collapse on my sisters, Mom, and me seventeen years ago? Mom didn't make it out alive.

Nah, it can't be him.

How is it possible? He'd given the landlord a false identity, and then he left the country to avoid going to prison. We expected him to be nowhere near France, or even Europe. Yet here he is in Provence, attending a party in a villa not far from Beldoc!

Was he at the party from the very beginning? Did he just walk in? Has he seen me? Does he know who I am? Will he recognize me?

A woman behind me asks if I can help her. I turn around to see what she needs. More apple crumble, as it turns out. She absolutely loved her first serving, and there seems to be none left on the cake table. Reassuring her that I have more in reserve, I dash to the kitchen. When I return with a ramekin for her, and a dozen for the cake bar, the contractor—or the man I mistook for him—is nowhere to be seen.

Did he step out for a smoke?

Did he go to the bathroom?

Did he leave?

If so, I should run out to see if I can catch up with him before he drives off. *But I can't.* We're catering. I'm the boss, and it is my job to make sure that this event ends as smoothly as it began.

~

THE MOST WANTED man on the Cavallo sisters' list never reappears.

It's soon two in the morning. The last bottle has been uncorked. All the pastries have been devoured. The last guests just walked out the door. While the hosts catch their breaths, we pack up and clean both the salon and the kitchen. The Ponsards' housekeeper will no doubt have the villa scrubbed again tomorrow morning, but that's all right. She'll be relieved to find out the ground floor doesn't look like a pigsty. She may recommend us to the housekeepers of the neighboring villas. And while she's at it, why not hire us to cater a celebration of her own.

When we're done cleaning, Valerie and Jean-Louis come to me with two bottles of muscatel they'd set aside, a check, and a generous tip in cash. They thank me for the impeccable evening. I thank them for the opportunity.

"Among your guests there was this tall man, late forties, dark hair, neat little beard with a bit of gray in it," I say. "Who is he?"

They seem to struggle to place him.

"What was he wearing?" Valerie asks.

"A well-cut suit, white shirt, no tie."

She smiles. "That was the uniform of half the men at the party."

"True." I glance at her similarly uniformed husband.

Also true that quite a few of the men at this party were tall and sported faux-casual stubble or a close-cropped beard.

She winks at me. "Was he alone?"

Oh no, she thinks I'm interested in him!

"It's not like that," I say. "He reminded me of someone from before my family left for Paris. I was just curious if it was the same person."

"I wish we could help you," Jean-Louis says.

How about you give me a copy of your guest list?

Thing is, even if I had the gall to ask for it, they wouldn't. Privacy rules in these circles.

"Never mind," I say. "It's not important."

Once our equipment and supplies have been transferred to Eric's minivan, Tino and Flo head to Tino's car.

"Hey," I call after them. "Do you mind if Flo rides back with us?"

Tino quirks an eyebrow. "Shop talk or investigation talk?"

"Shop talk," I lie.

Shooting me a quizzical glance, Flo makes a U-turn to the minivan.

As soon as we're on the road, I tell Flo and Eric about the mystery man I saw at the party, and his uncanny resemblance to the contractor in my snapshot. As part of FERJ, Eric knows about my visions. He also knows about what happened at the beach house seventeen years ago.

I conclude my report with a self-directed rant, "I'm so mad at myself for letting him slip away!"

"Don't beat yourself up, Chef," Eric comforts me. "We now know he's back in France."

"Hiding in plain sight, right under our noses!" Flo exclaims.

"This guy must be a chameleon, someone that routinely changes his appearance to avoid getting caught," I say.

Flo and Eric nod.

"And his name, too," Flo adds. "We know from the meager info the police have on him that the name he used to sign the refurbishment contract for the beach house was fake."

From the driver's seat, Eric throws me a glance. "Do you think Gabriel would be able to help us?"

It's a surprisingly tricky question to answer, partly because I don't know how much of the gendarmerie resources he can tap into, and partly because—

"Gabriel doesn't know about any of this, does he?" Flo asks me.

There's an uncharacteristic note of compassion in her tone.

"No," I admit. "Does Tino know?"

"Nope."

"Some things are harder to share with a lover than with a friend," Eric observes.

While I do agree with the point, I can't resist teasing him, "Is that quote from Mr. Spock or Captain Kirk?"

All of Eric's life lessons are drawn from *Star Trek*.

"Neither of them, for once," he replies with a chuckle. "It's all mine."

Flo feigns amazement. "So much wisdom in one so young!"

"We're the same age," he reminds her.

"My soul is older," she counters.

That's cheeky, considering all the personal drama Eric has been through. Unless, of course, Flo meant it in a karmic, reincarnational sense. Which, being Rose's most like-minded granddaughter, she probably did.

CHAPTER 16

Gabriel and I are driving home from a lovely evening in Arles. He's tuned in a radio channel playing some great folk rock. Hands on the steering wheel and eyes on the road, he looks all happy and relaxed.

I feel guilty about bringing up homicide, but I've been delaying my question all evening. It has to come out.

"Do you expect Leon Rapp to be found guilty of his brother's murder?"

His expression becomes weary. "Must we talk about it now? We were having such a fun time!"

"It's important to me."

He lets out a resigned sigh. "Leon claims he was alone in his bed when Horace was attacked."

"Which means he has no alibi, right?"

"Correct." He turns the music down. "All evidence, both circumstantial and direct, points to Leon. Besides, he had not one but two motives, according to Loubardin."

"Greed being the first one?"

"By removing Horace, Leon was pocketing Coralie's

inheritance plus Horace's own assets," Gabriel says. "That's a strong motive."

"And the second one was jealousy or envy that Yoona had chosen Horace, wasn't it?"

"Not exactly."

"Oh?"

He wiggles his eyebrows. "It was a love triangle drama."

"Tell me more!"

"Turns out Leon wasn't just carrying a torch for Yoona while she dated Horace. She'd slept with him, too."

"How... artistic!" I say.

"Ever since she arrived in town, she'd been torturing the Rapp brothers. She started off seeing Horace, then tried Leon, and then went back to Horace."

"Wow, a true heartbreaker!"

His shoulders rise and drop. "Women."

"Do you think the investigators in Arles will reopen Coralie Bray's case?" I ask. "You know, in light of what happened."

"Maybe. Or maybe not. The cases aren't necessarily linked."

"Oh, come on!" I angle my body toward him as much as the seat belt will let me. "If Leon was capable of eliminating his brother, isn't it probable he'd killed the aunt?"

"Possible, not probable. The verdict is she died from a stroke caused by excessive chiropractic adjustment."

"Wasn't the ME's report inconclusive?"

Gabriel nods.

I carry on, "What if Leon had given her some delayed onset poison to cause a stroke?"

"Wasn't your earlier theory that Horace had poisoned her?"

"It was," I admit. "Leon seemed too nice, too friendly... But I've changed my mind now."

He's about to react when something happening by the roadside diverts his attention. I follow his gaze. A gendarmerie car is parked behind a battered Dacia Duster. A group consisting of uniformed gendarmes and dolled-up civilians are discussing something on the other side of the emergency strip.

Gabriel pulls over behind them and unfastens his belt. "Let me see what this is about."

"I'm coming with you," I say, unbuckling mine.

He doesn't try to stop me. He knows me well enough by now to realize nothing can stop me when my curiosity has been piqued.

As we approach the group, I make out two young men with bloodstains on their dress shirts, two young women, and an older man and woman. The younger bunch appears drunk. Taking a closer look at the young men, I realize that the bloodstains on their shirts aren't from gunshots or stab wounds but from split lips and perhaps a broken tooth or two. They're brandishing their fists and calling each other nasty names. If it weren't for the gendarmes restraining them, they'd be swapping punches again.

Gabriel and the gendarmes exchange friendly greetings. The uniforms clearly know him, but I've never met them before.

"This is Julie, a friend," he introduces me.

A. Friend. Someday soon, I'm going to confront him about that.

"What's going on?" he asks his colleagues.

"It's a tricky situation," one of them says. "This group had to leave a wedding party because the brothers,"—he points out the young men with bloodied shirts—"got drunk and started fighting."

"OK." Gabriel nods.

The gendarme continues, "They'd both been hitting on

some hot chick during the party, so the girlfriends are mad at them."

Two brothers vying for the same woman? I've heard that tale before...

"Wait, there's more," another gendarme says, pointing at one of the young women. "This lady here is so pissed she's threatening to claw her boyfriend's eyes out."

"Perhaps she means it figuratively?" I venture.

He gives me an "I wish" look. "She tried to execute her threat a few minutes ago."

I glance at her manicured nails. They're so long they curve inward.

Gabriel follows my gaze. "I'm beginning to understand your predicament."

"The brothers' father, Monsieur Dorsi, had to pull over because the fighting between his sons and their girlfriends turned into a brawl, and they were putting themselves and others on the road at risk."

Gabriel turns to Monsieur Dorsi. "That was a responsible thing to do. Bravo!"

"Yeah, but what do I do now?" the man appeals to him, distressed. "How do I get everyone home?"

"Two cabs," Gabriel suggests. "You put the girlfriends into one, your wife with one of your sons in the other, and you drive the remaining son home in your car."

"A half-hour drive to our town in two taxis, at the insane night rate?" Monsieur Dorsi wags his index finger. "We don't have that kind of money."

"We offered to drop the boys off at the drunk tank in the nearest gendarmerie," the uniformed gendarme says to Gabriel. "But Madame Dorsi is strongly opposed to that idea."

"No son of mine is spending the night in the drunk tank!" she cries out.

Her husband inquires of the gendarme, "Why don't you drive one of them to our house, and I'll follow with the other?"

"We're on patrol, Monsieur," the gendarme replies. "We've spent far too long here already."

The nonviolent girlfriend starts to sob. "I just want to go hooome!"

Everybody turns to Gabriel, as if expecting him to solve their quagmire. I wonder if it's because he has an air of authority about him, which I'm immune to. Or is it because he outranks the uniforms? Or maybe it's just the way he swept in, the providential man.

Well, chéri, you better not disappoint them!

He flashes a palm in warning. "Give me a sec. I need to think."

Everybody shuts up so he can think, even the insult-spewing brothers and the wailing girlfriend.

"What we have here," Gabriel says, "is a wolf, goat, and cabbage situation."

Everybody gives him a blank stare.

"Don't you guys know it?" He looks from me to the gendarmes to the stranded family.

We shake our heads.

"Never mind." He closes his eyes for another moment.

Now I'm *really* curious to hear his solution.

"Monsieur Dorsi can get everyone home safely, if he makes two trips," Gabriel says, opening his eyes. They sparkle with roguish triumph.

"Care to elaborate, *mon Capitaine?*" the first gendarme asks.

"Monsieur Dorsi cannot take his sons' girlfriends first, because if his sons wait here, they'll start fighting again, and their mother may not be able to stop them," Gabriel says.

"Nor can he begin with the couple with the lady who threatened to hurt his son."

"So, who do I take first?" Monsieur Dorsi asks.

"You take both young ladies and the son whose eyes aren't under threat," Gabriel says. "Your wife will wait here with your other son. Then you'll come back and collect them."

The solution seems to satisfy the turbulent family. As Monsieur Dorsi peels away with the first batch, so do we.

"Good thinking there," I compliment him.

He keeps his eyes on the road, looking pleased. "I try."

This is as good a time as it will ever be to hit him with my favor. "Can you arrange for me to meet with the lead investigator in the Coralie Bray case?"

"Julie—"

"Please! I just want to plead with him to reconsider Quentin's guilt, that's all."

After a few seconds of silence, he nods. "I'll reach out to him."

We don't discuss anything murder related after that.

CHAPTER 17

Commissaire Anjara's office is small and drafty with few pieces of furniture and a color scheme exclusively in shades of gray and brown. I advance to the well-worn wooden desk. It's as tidy and minimalistic as the rest of the office, save for a neat stack of files, a cardboard box, and a wallet-sized picture of a smiling family.

Behind the desk, a graying man wearing a gray suit gestures to the chair in front of him. "Hello, Madame Cavallo. Please have a seat."

I sit down. Anjara's piercing black eyes drill into me. Unwilling to defy him with an equally unfriendly gaze, I study the zigzagging crack across the ceiling, the window looking out onto the street, and the bare walls. One wall isn't bare. It hosts a cork board, with notes pinned to it, a framed degree, sepia maps of Madagascar and France, and an impeccably aligned row of commendations.

"You have my undivided attention for the next ten minutes," he finally says.

I level my eyes with his. "You've heard about Horace Rapp's murder and Leon Rapp's arrest, haven't you?"

"Yes. I've also heard you delivered some damning evidence."

I straighten in my chair. "I did."

"Capitaine Adinian tells me you're convinced Quentin Vernet is innocent of any wrongdoing. Is he a friend of yours?"

"Friend of a friend."

He puts his elbows on the desk and leans forward. "What exactly do you want from me, Madame Cavallo?"

"Please, reopen the Coralie Bray case."

"On what basis?"

"On the basis that Quentin may be innocent because someone—likely Leon Rapp—had poisoned Coralie shortly before her chiropractic treatment."

He pulls the cardboard box closer, opens it and starts sifting through the manila files, envelopes, and loose sheets held together by a paper clip. I wait patiently until I realize he isn't going to react to my statement.

But I'm not one to give up easily. "What say you, Commissaire? Isn't that a new and relevant element that's compelling enough to reconsider your earlier conclusions?"

"Everything I learned about the Rapp brothers and their relationship with their aunt makes it extremely improbable that one or both of them would attempt to kill her," he finally says, lifting his eyes from the box. "She was like a mother to them."

"People kill their mothers, too."

He returns his attention to the box. A moment later, he pulls out a folder, opens it, and picks up a stapled document. "This here is the ME's report. I wish the findings were more specific, but they are consistent with Quentin Vernet's conviction for medical malpractice."

"And yet, like you just said, the findings aren't specific enough."

Again, no reaction.

I draw a breath to keep my voice calm and untainted by resentment. "I've done some research on fatal chiropractic mistakes. They are exceptionally rare."

Anjara curls his lip in annoyance. "Believe me, dear Madame, I have done my research too."

"Then you'll agree with my statement."

"I will not." He sits back and crosses his arms. "The estimated occurrences vary wildly."

He isn't making that up. I've seen that variance, and even Quentin spoke of it. Obviously, it's the lowest estimate that I chose to go with.

Anjara brings his head up. "The expert that testified at the hearing told the court that most cases go unreported because the stroke or the heart attack comes days later. The victim or their family simply don't realize there may be a link."

I search his face, scrambling for another argument.

Is he really sticking to his guns, despite the major recent development? Am I losing this battle?

Desperate, I point at the box. "Do you have the full autopsy report with the raw data and all?"

"I do. Why?"

"May I have a copy?"

"You may not."

"All right." I shift in my seat. "May I at least ask you to look at the actual data? See if it's maybe consistent with poisoning?"

"If it were, don't you think the ME would've flagged it in his conclusions?"

"I suppose so..." I press my palms together in entreaty, even as in my mind, I'm already making peace with defeat.

"Please? All I'm asking is that you look when you get a chance."

To my utter surprise, he throws his hands up. "You know what? I'll do it right now, right here, before this box goes back to the records room."

He sets the folder on his desk and retrieves a thick document, which he begins to peruse, sliding the tip of his index finger down lines and lines of scientific terms and numeric values.

I watch him intently at first.

He mutters, "Normal... normal... normal..." as he turns pages.

My mind begins to wander off.

"Alcohol... narcotics... heavy metals..." He looks up at me. "She was tested for neurotoxins, too. Just to show you how thorough we were."

He returns to the data and the mumbling.

I turn away and gaze out the window. Quentin will be heartbroken. I gave him hope and then failed him. I should've listened to Gabriel and Rose and given this case a pass.

Anjara falls silent. He must've finished the report. I turn to him, opening my mouth to apologize for wasting his time, when I realize he isn't on the last page yet. He's about halfway through the report and staring at something that's making his left eyelid twitch.

"What is it?" I ask. "Did you find something?"

He leafs through to an earlier section, checks something out, and then returns to his latest data point. His foot is now jerking, too, the heel tapping a rapid staccato on the floor.

"What?" I ask again.

"She'd been taking an MAOI—"

"Come again?"

"A class of antidepressants," he explains. "Alone it's not a problem. But the biochemistry of those drugs makes it dangerous to consume certain other meds and foods in conjunction with them."

"What happens if one does?"

"Blood pressure may shoot up and the person may"—he swallows hard before finishing his sentence—"suffer a hemorrhagic stroke."

"Did Coralie Bray consume any of those other meds or foods?"

"According to this report, she had a high concentration of caffeine in her blood. It was sublethal, all right, and again, not an issue by itself. But, given the presence of the MAOI... this may suggest..." He gasps for air.

"That she died from a drug interaction or was poisoned," I finish for him.

He hangs his head.

Tilting my head to the side, I search his face. "How could the ME leave that out from the summary report?"

"Clearly, he'd missed the connection."

I hate to gloat, but I can't help remarking, "If you hadn't gone into the case prejudiced against chiropractors, *you* may have spotted it earlier."

"It wasn't prejudice."

"Then what?"

"I guess I over-relied on my instincts, which had never let me down before." He glances at the commendations on the wall. "My gut screamed that Quentin Vernet was guilty."

"Well, your gut was wrong."

I say no more aloud, but the unspoken truth is glaring at us from the autopsy report. He overlooked a crucial piece of information. As a result, an innocent man served time. That innocent man also lost his license, his good name, and his livelihood.

Anjara stands up abruptly. "Will you excuse me, Madame

Cavallo? I must speak with the ME and then with the magistrate."

"Of course."

Off you go to fix your fuckup!

He motions me to the door. "And, please, do not tell the whole world about this just yet. The case will likely be reopened, and we must protect the investigation."

"I understand," I say, heading for the exit. "But don't wait too long."

CHAPTER 18

The Refractory Gaul up on Butte Royale is arguably Beldoc's trendiest and most expensive restaurant. It's here that Quentin decided we celebrate his deliverance. I tried to talk him out of his choice, but nothing doing.

We are gently ushered into the main dining room. It's the way I remember it from two years ago with subdued indirect lighting, slate floors, pale wood, and starched white napkins. I sniff the air, trying to figure out what the chef is cooking tonight. It's hard to tell. Or rather, I'm picking up several contradictory notes that confuse my brain.

The maître d' leads us through the front room to the table Quentin has booked on the vine-covered terrace in the backyard. The ladies—Rose, Flo, and me—are offered the seats looking at the terrace, while the gentlemen—Eric, Salman, and Quentin—face the wall. I'm all for feminism and equal rights, but I do enjoy a bit of old-fashioned male gallantry every now and then. Luckily, it still survives here in the South.

"Are you familiar with our concept?" the maître d' asks us.

Everybody shakes their heads.

Denis brought me here once during my first months back in Beldoc, but things may have changed since then.

"All our ingredients are grown locally," he says. "Most are organic. We have wines from the best local vineyards, but also from other regions of France and Italy."

"I'm assuming you serve French cuisine?" Rose asks. "Judging by the name of the place."

"Our menu is a mixture of traditional and innovative dishes," the maître d' says. "It varies seasonally and depends on the chef's mood."

She puts her hands on her knees. "What's his mood like today?"

"Mysterious," he replies, retreating.

A server takes his place. He sets a basket of sliced baguette and portions of salted butter on the table. After handing out elegant black holders with today's menu, he leaves.

While we study the menu, an accordionist in a 1950s jacket and a black hat settles in the musicians' corner of the terrace. I love the accordion, but I worry we'll have to shout over it during the meal. It's always the case in the truck kitchen *guinguette* places that pop up along the riverbank every summer.

But my fears evaporate when the accordionist starts to play. His sound is sweetly retro and soft enough that it's possible to enjoy a conversation without raising your voice.

We're not in a guinguette anymore, Toto! That said, the menu prices alone, none of them in single digits except the espresso shot, leave no doubt in that regard.

"You and I are splitting the bill," I say to Quentin.

"Three ways." Salman turns to his friend. "If you foot this

alone, you'll be eating naked pasta on weekdays and plain rice on weekends for the rest of the month."

Quentin juts his chin out. "Not happening."

Rose swats his hand from across the table. "Be reasonable, boy."

"Now that Coralie's case was reopened," Quentin says, "there will be a retrial. It's almost certain I'll be acquitted. I'll recover my license and my practice, and I'll get damages for my wrongful imprisonment."

"But all of that will take time," I argue.

"Julie, none of it would've been possible without you and your friends." Quentin sweeps his hand around the table. "So, yes, I insist. It's the least I can do."

The server reappears and takes our orders, including champagne for aperitif, on Quentin's demand.

As soon as the bubbly is served, Salman proposes a toast. "To yet another case solved by FERJ!"

"Not quite," I object.

He wrinkles his nose at me. "Don't be such a spoilsport! We don't have the verdicts yet, but it's obvious what they'll be."

"Quentin will be acquitted of medical malpractice, and Leon will be convicted of his brother's murder," Rose says.

"When you were talking to that commissaire over in Arles… What was his name again?" Flo asks.

"Anjara."

"Right, Anjara. Did you get a sense that he'll really go after Leon for Coralie's poisoning?" She fidgets with her napkin. "Or will he deliver minimum service just to close that pesky case?"

I give her question some thought. "I basically watched him realize the fuckup in real time as he went through the data. He was genuinely shocked."

"Besides," Eric chimes in, "the fact that he admitted the oversight in front of you speaks to his goodwill."

Quentin rolls his eyes. "Goodwill, my ass."

"You have every reason to despise him," Eric says to Quentin. "Having been in your shoes, dealing with an officer convinced of my guilt, I do relate, believe me."

Quentin tilts his head. "But?"

"But…" Eric pauses, choosing his words. "But you can't deny that his behavior during his conversation with Julie shows a certain degree of integrity."

"I agree," Salman says. "When he saw the proof of poisoning in the raw data, he didn't have to tell Julie about it."

Flo turns toward me. "Could you see the data from where you sat?"

"Yes. But I stopped looking after page two. It was meaningless to me."

She nods. "So Anjara could've easily said nothing to Julie, and then raised the matter with the ME, or asked his superiors for advice."

"By acknowledging the oversight in front of Julie, he crossed the point of no return," Salman says.

Rose chimes in, "He made sure the police wouldn't be able to cover it up and act like there was no problem with the autopsy findings."

Quentin harrumphs but doesn't argue against our consensus.

The appetizers arrive. It's a mix of Provençale specialties and Mediterranean dishes, including beef carpaccio, two kinds of tapenade on toast, pissaladière topped with anchovies and onions, and burrata with pesto.

"So, let's recap," Eric says, digging into his carpaccio. "Coralie Bray was poisoned in her house, just before she left for her session with Quentin."

"It seems like the most probable scenario," I agree. "One of her nephews, most probably Leon, slipped some crushed pills and pure caffeine powder in her tea."

Quentin's eyebrows shoot up. "What makes you say it was tea?"

Neither he nor Salman knows about my snapshots, and I have no intention of telling them now. Which puts me in a bind. How do I tell Quentin that I know Coralie complained about her tea tasting funny without telling him I saw it in a vision?

"I'm just assuming she was a tea drinker, given her age," I lie. "But it could've been coffee, or any other beverage. Or food."

Rose shakes her head. "Where would I be if people assumed things about me based on my age?"

"You'd have no doga students, and you wouldn't be Queen of Beldoc, that's for sure!" Flo says to chuckles and cheers.

Our server returns to clear the table and replace the silver. A colleague of his brings the mains, which are as easy on the eyes as they are on the nose. We fall silent while the servers do their thing, focusing our attention on the accordionist playing a Piaf tune.

But my mind isn't at ease. No matter how hard I try, I can't shake the feeling that something about this case doesn't compute. It isn't one big thing, or even one medium-sized thing, but a combination of small things. Taken separately, each can be easily written off. But together, they make me wonder.

After a good deal of weighing the pros and cons of speaking my mind, I decide to go for it. "Why wasn't Leon wearing a cap that morning, when he set bees on Horace? He took care to hide his face but left his very recognizable hair uncovered."

No one answers.

"And why on earth didn't he dispose of Horace's EpiPen away from the house?" I plow on. "Why bring it home and toss it in his own trash?"

"Help! She's bringing up the too-sloppy execution again." Rose sets her fork and knife down and gives me a weary look. "People are dumb. They do dumb things. All. The. Time."

Unexpectedly, Flo takes my side. "Something about Coralie's murder bugs me, too. How much did the siblings expect to inherit, in addition to the house she'd already given them? She was a PA all her life. It can't be that much."

"And, given that both Horace and Leon had decent-paying jobs," I add, "and that their aunt doted on them, what was their reason for poisoning her?"

"They loved her, too, from what we've learned through our research," Eric says.

I feel like hugging both of them right now. Maybe they're only saying this because I'm their boss, but I don't care. It's good not to be the only killjoy ruining Quentin's celebration.

Eric continues, "She looked after her nephews when her sister—their mom—became ill and died. She invited them to live in her specifically redone house, rent free..."

"Which reminds me." I tilt my head to one side. "How was she able to afford that kind of generosity?"

"Perhaps she lived above her means," Rose offers. "Perhaps her nephews, too, lived above their means and accumulated huge credit card debt. Which means they were desperate for money."

You know a thing or two about that, don't you?

I notice how Eric and Flo avert their eyes from Rose. They must be thinking the same thing.

"One of them could've had gambling debts," she persists.

"Or drug-related debts, or anything that put one or both of the brothers in urgent need of cash."

"Except, so far we've seen nothing to suggest they have debts," I say.

Everybody falls silent, sipping their wine.

I can't get rid of the feeling we're missing something. Something like a big gorilla in the middle of a room that nobody notices because it's so out of place. Because nobody expects to see it. But once they do, they realize how obvious it was, and they wonder how they could've missed it.

When the waiters return with the cheese trolley that they push around the table for everyone to pick their cheeses, I make up my mind.

"I'm going to visit Leon in jail," I announce.

Rose goggles at me. "What will you tell him? Hey, I'm the gal that got you that lovely room for your extended taxpayer-sponsored vacation?"

"I'll air my doubts with him," I say. "What's the worst that can happen?"

Eric's brow constricts. "He'll refuse to talk to you, Chef."

"Or he'll shout abuse at you," Flo warns me.

"But what if he hears me out?" I survey their discouraging miens. "What if he talks to me?"

"Then he'll lie," Salman says.

"His lies may give us a new perspective on his motives…" My voice trails off, as I nearly give up in the face of such a lack of support.

"You should give it a shot," Quentin says to my surprise. "Who knows, maybe there really is more to this story than meets the eye."

CHAPTER 19

I bet it's easier to get the Michelin Guide to publish a glowing review—not that I ever had the honor—than to obtain a permit to visit a suspect in pretrial detention. I played the "I'm trying to help the investigation" card, and the "by the way, I've already helped this investigation" card, even the "I've solved murders before" card. But to no avail. Begging Capitaine Loubardin was what did the trick in the end. Sort of. He begrudgingly agreed to ask Leon if he'd talk to me on the phone.

I've been waiting to hear from Loubardin with Leon's reply since yesterday.

It's the middle of the afternoon now, the second quietest hour at the shop. We're done in the lab for now, having made two strawberry tarts from a recipe Eric wanted to try, and some chocolate truffles. With no customers to serve at the moment, Eric is refreshing our website and compiling this week's newsletter. I'm ordering supplies.

Outside the window, Karl plants his folding stool under the oak tree. His ever-happy dog, Harley, stretches out beside him. It's very warm, so Karl removes the pungent bomber jacket he's had on his back from April through October. The faded T-shirt underneath reveals just how hollowed his chest is.

Our eyes meet, and I nod to let him know the treat is coming. Back when a urinal still graced the sidewalk in front of Magda's shop, she and I struck a deal with Karl. He refrained from using that urinal by day, and we made sure he had a coffee and a croissant when he turned up.

With the urinal gone, the deal is void. But unless I'm too busy, I still indulge him. To show his gratitude, he doesn't stay long, minimizing the loss of potential customers, too squeamish about body odors.

I step out with a coffee and a brioche for him. "What's up, Karl?"

"Inflation. Economy down. Folks worry about the future and hold on to their money." He points at his empty coin cup.

"Can you maybe find a job?" I ask. "Does the guy who had you selling chestnuts at the Christmas market have a summer opportunity?"

Karl shakes his head. "He'll rehire me when the market is back up in November."

"Can you maybe sell ice cream in the meantime?"

"There aren't many people who want to hire me," he says.

"I'll vouch for you—"

"To be honest, I'm not that eager, either." He bites into his brioche. "I quite enjoy the slower pace."

Ah. "Because you're still burned out from roasting chestnuts?"

He nods. In all seriousness.

O-okay, then. "But, tell me, don't you get bored doing nothing all day?"

Another nod. "I wish I could read. I used to read a lot."

"Why did you stop?"

"My eyesight got worse with age."

"Have you tried reading glasses?"

"Yeah," he says. "They work great. But the cheapest cost something like fifteen euros. I can't afford it."

"Your *sécurité sociale* should cover a pair of reading glasses."

He shrugs. "Maybe. I don't know. I lost my card, and sort of fell through the cracks."

I dash to the door and tell Eric I'll be back in half an hour.

"Come with me," I say to Karl in my bossiest tone. "There's a pharmacy at the end of the street that sells reading glasses. They'll help you pick the right pair, and I'll pay for it."

Without discussion, he swallows the rest of his coffee and breaks camp.

Fifteen minutes later, we exit the pharmacy with Karl carrying a pair of sturdy plastic-rimmed glasses in his pocket.

"I really appreciate it, Julie," he says. "What can I do to thank you?"

It's very tempting to suggest that he find a homeless shelter where he can shower more often. Rose would've said it. But I'm not Rose. Not yet, at any rate.

"That's all right." I pet Harley, preparing to add that I'm happy he'll pick up a book again, when my phone rings.

It's Loubardin. "Leon Rapp said yes, whatever."

"He'll talk to me? Oh great! When?"

"One option is right now, actually."

I glance at Karl. "Yes, fine, put him through."

Karl waves goodbye, and I head to a spot by the wall that's out of the way.

When Leon's voice sounds on my phone, it's both

familiar and different. The pitch and inflections are the same as when I took Lady for a grooming session. But there's such a bleak dullness to his tone now that you'd think he aged two decades in a week.

I begin by telling him why I was spying on Horace, and that his aunt's case was reopened. From his lack of reaction, I conclude he's already heard. Assuming Leon is the one that poisoned her, he can't be pleased about that news. Lucky for him, our system doesn't believe in consecutive sentences. I'm not sure he'll stay longer in jail for a double homicide than for a single murder.

"Are you satisfied?" he asks when I run out of things to say.

"That an innocent man's name will be cleared? Yes."

"How do you know he's innocent?"

Did he listen while I was talking? "Your aunt had been poisoned."

"Poisoned with what?"

"I'm not supposed to tell you."

He lets out a bitter laugh. "Here I am, behind bars, accused of killing my brother, and a prime suspect in my aunt's murder... How is it even possible?"

"You mean you thought you'd never get caught?"

"I mean I didn't kill anyone!" he yells suddenly.

There's so much anger and emotion in his voice, that it seems feigned... like he's overacting.

"All I ever wanted to do with my life," he says, "was take care of living things. Plants, animals, humans. And now I'm accused of killing people. My own kin! That's just... unimaginable."

OK, so he claims he's innocent. Good. That's something. I can work with that.

"There are things about your aunt's case that puzzle me," I begin. "Like, for instance, her being able to afford such a major remodel of her house and letting you and Horace live there without paying rent."

"Believe it or not, I asked her the exact same questions, many times."

"What did she say?" I begin pacing, too eager to stand still. "How did she explain away her wealth?"

"She told me she'd been saving all her life, and that she got a very generous retirement package from her last company."

"The pharma start-up in Arles?"

"Yes, SivryMed. Aunt Coralie was a PA to the head of R & D, Ines Kabbaj, who appreciated her professionalism and discretion so much that she wanted it rewarded."

"Discretion?"

"It's a pharma company," he reminds me.

Hmm. Up until this moment, I only thought of Coralie Bray as a recently retired senior with back issues and two nephews. But the truth is, she was more than that. She'd been a working woman all her life, and she'd had relationships and connections, and perhaps conflicts, linked to the preretirement phase of her life. A phase that needs a closer look than we've given it so far.

"Did she have enemies?" I ask Leon. "Perhaps, someone at SivryMed or a company she worked at before? Someone who hated her with a passion?"

"I don't think so. If such a person existed, I would've heard about them."

Another idea occurs to me. "Did she know things about her boss or a previous boss or someone else that would've damaged that person's reputation if she revealed them?"

"You mean hush money?" He gives a snort. "Yeah, it's a theory I had. I kept asking her if the CEO, Paul Sivry, or her direct boss, Ines, was cheating on their respective spouses, or something like that."

"And?"

"She always laughed it off, and after her death, we found nothing to corroborate that theory."

Aha, another thread I pull on! "So, you and Horace searched the house after she died?"

"Of course."

"Did you find anything at all that seemed out of place or suspicious? Compromising photos or letters? Copies of financial documents?"

"The only compromising photo we found was of Aunt Coralie, skinny-dipping with her friends when she was twenty."

"What about her finances?" I ask. "Did you discover a million euros sitting in her bank account?"

"She had some money, but nothing remotely close to a million."

"And her bank statements?"

"Horace combed through them. He didn't find anything weird."

"Did you tell the cops about your theory?" I ask.

"What's the point? I have nothing to support it."

"Still," I say, "you should share your thoughts with Capitaine Loubardin."

He laughs a joyless laugh. "And, just like that, you're on my side?"

"I'm on the side of the truth," I point out, bristling.

"Have you seen Yoona recently?" he asks without a transition, his tone losing all trace of sarcasm.

"No, why?"

"She's put in a request for a visit, but they told her she'll have to wait until after the trial." He swears under his breath. "I worry about her."

"I met her only briefly, but she struck me as a very resourceful person."

"That, she is! She has so much talent, and great business acumen, and she's so…" He inhales sharply. "I'm sorry."

"That's all right."

"It's just the thought that I'll never be with her…" He snuffles. "You'll laugh, but I find it as hard to bear as being accused of Horace's murder."

"I understand, Leon."

"Horace and I were at war trying to win her heart, to be the one she'll marry…"

"Don't lose heart just yet."

"It's hard not to," he says. "Horace is dead now, because somebody wanted him gone, for whatever reason. And I'll rot behind bars because that same person framed me."

I mutter words of encouragement and tell him he should be strong and keep faith. Even as I speak those words, I'm reminding myself to not fall for Leon's tricks. He's a proficient liar. And a murderer.

But what if he isn't?

In that case, Leon is in a hole so deep it makes Quentin's year in prison look like a joke.

After we hang up, a rather disturbing thought strikes me. Let's assume for a moment that Leon is innocent. What does that make me? That makes me a useful idiot who unwittingly helped the killer.

CHAPTER 20

Rose, Magda, Igor, and I have an appointment with Victor in his office at the town hall at nine in the morning. Magda and Igor had submitted all the required documents for a permit to convert Tatiana's restaurant into retail and split it into two shops. Tatiana is fully on board with the plan. They have a solid case, but the administration tends to be overly suspicious of projects involving too much change, which makes success hit or miss.

Because Tatiana is stuck in Nantes where she has a job now, Rose will represent her. And I will cheer Team Magda. In the unlikely event that Victor green-lights the project, she'll satisfy her itch to extend Lavender Dream. In which case, seeing me go bankrupt and disappear will hopefully cease to be her short-term goal.

It's now eight in the morning.

Gabriel and I just walked out of my building. He'll be off on an assignment later today, returning next Tuesday. With that prospect in sight, neither of us is in a hurry to say goodbye and go about our daily business. I guess that's why

THE BLOODTHIRSTY BEE

he broke his vow of discretion and asked if he could tag along until Place de la Mairie.

We walk in silence for a while. Last night, I told him about my conversation with Leon. His reaction was, "I hope you didn't believe a word he said." At that point, I didn't have the nerve to tell him the truth. But I do now.

"I'm going to pay a visit to SivryMed, the pharma start-up where Coralie worked before her retirement," I announce.

He gives me a long, heavy-lidded look. "A pharma boss kills an employee to protect a dirty secret. He frames an innocent man for it. A year later, he kills again, and frames another innocent man for it, just because he can. Did I get your new theory right?"

"When you put it like that..." I exhale, rattling my lips.

But he presses on. "Why, what's the issue? Does it sound less convincing this morning than yesterday when Leon Rapp planted it in your head?"

"Calling him was my initiative."

"Julie." He stops and turns to face me. "You must walk away from that case. You've done your part."

"But I still have questions, and there are gaps and inconsistencies—"

"Leave them to the cops. Loubardin is on Horace Rapp's case, and Anjara has reopened Coralie Bray's. Let them do their work."

"Anjara had mucked it up with Quentin." I purse my lips.

"Which is why he'll be extra careful this time around." Gabriel's gaze bores into mine. "Please. I'll be away for a week, and I want you to promise me you'll drop it."

I keep my lips pressed together and don't respond.

"Please, *bébé*, tell me that when I walk in through your door next Tuesday, we won't be talking about the Rapp brothers!"

"How about we meet in the barracks when you're back?" I suggest, surprising myself. "I'd like to hang out in your apartment for a change."

He lets go of my hand. "That's a bad idea."

"But why?" I fidget with the bracelet he gave me.

He runs his hand over the lower half of his face, his visage conflicted.

"When I joined the Beldoc Brigade," he finally says, "I became pals with another lieutenant, Raphael Morillot. We worked together, watched sports together, played the same videogames, enjoyed the same movies…"

"Sounds like a bromance."

"It was!" His mouth skews a smile. "The others teased us about it. But we didn't care. It was the kind of friendship you cherish because it's a gift."

"Was he transferred away?"

"He met a lovely woman during my second year in Beldoc. They were married within months, and then a baby came."

I sneer. "Let me guess—it killed your bromance."

"Not really. I liked her. She was fun. It's true, I saw Raphael a lot less outside of work, but our friendship remained just as solid."

He falls silent, lost in thought.

"What happened to him?" I ask, sensing that this story doesn't have a happy ending. "Did he get killed?

"No."

Even as I'm sighing with relief, Gabriel adds, "It was his wife that got killed."

"How?"

"Raphael was investigating a corruption case that involved some high-ranking officials and influential businessmen. He was getting close, too close…"

I press my hand to my breastbone. "Did those people have Raphael's wife killed to intimidate him?"

"He got a call from the day care center one evening, because his wife hadn't shown up. He picked up the kid, took him home. His wife wasn't there. She wasn't at her workplace, either."

I brace myself for the rest of it.

"The next day," Gabriel says, "her dead body was found in a wasteland outside of Beldoc. She'd been shot in the head. There was a note shoved into her pocket. A warning that the boy would be next."

"What did Raphael do?"

"He quit the gendarmerie, took his son, and moved to Spain to his grandparents' village."

"Was the killer ever found?" I peer into his eyes. "Did the gendarmerie follow up on Raphael's leads?"

"I started doing that, until I was ordered to stop."

"By your commandant?"

"He merely relayed the order. It had come from higher up."

For long seconds, we stare at each other in silence.

"Is that why you want me to drop the Horace Rapp case?" I ask him. "Because the thread I'm pulling may lead me to people that are too powerful and too dangerous?"

He shakes his head. "There's no thread, Julie. Leon lied to you on the off chance you could help him get off the hook."

I look away, unconvinced.

"I told you about Raphael," he says, "so you'd understand who I am, and how I live now. My folks aren't allowed to visit me in Beldoc. I love them to bits, but I tell everyone we're estranged. And I certainly don't want the whole town to know you and I are an item."

"And the whole town will know if I show up at the barracks?"

"The barracks are like a dorm," he says. "Only with apartments instead of rooms."

"That bad?"

"The moment you set foot in the building, someone's bound to spot you. And then all the wives and live-in girlfriends will want to meet you. And then the whole town will know you're with me."

I rock on my heels. "Surely, you exaggerate."

"Not at all. I want you to be safe, Julie."

The air between us has become so fraught that I feel compelled to lighten it. "With your evil eye bracelet on my wrist all day long, I'm super safe, thank you very much."

He responds with a look that's both smug and pleading, part James Bond and part Puss in Boots. "Will you drop the case?"

"I'll think about it." Glancing at my watch, I tug at his sleeve. "Hurry! One shouldn't keep the mayor waiting when one needs something from him."

∼

THE TOWN HALL has a musty smell of decaying wood about it, no doubt due to the central staircase that looks like something built under the *ancien régime*.

We follow Rose up the steps and down the corridor to a massive door at the end. Without knocking, she pushes it open.

Chantal, Victor's faithful PA looks up from her desk and points her chin to a second door on her right. "Go on, he's waiting for you."

As we enter, I take in Victor's spacious and sparsely furnished office. It's neither too shabby nor too fancy, and it smells better than the rest of the building. Must be because the window is wide open, and the sunny freshness of the morning neutralizes dust and mold.

Magda plants herself in the middle of the room, with her head high and her arms akimbo. Next to her, Rose mimics her body language. Standing beside Rose, I, too, put my chin up and prop my hands on my hips. Igor adopts a friendlier and more peaceful stance, the only one that makes sense, as it happens.

Magda cuts a glance at the gaping window and then at Victor's face. Her eyes sparkle with defiance as if she were throwing down the gauntlet.

This reminds me of their strife over the public urinal Victor had installed in front of Magda's shop a year ago. On that memorable occasion, Magda stormed his office and assaulted him with an endless string of choice epithets shouted so loud that half of the town could hear her.

Victor follows Magda's gaze. I expect him to dash to the window and close it, but he remains in his seat.

Considering that he knows what our visit is about, do I dare to interpret his failure to insulate the outside world against Magda's potential attack as a good sign? Or, on the contrary, is it a dare of his own, a statement that he won't be intimidated by Magda's yelling?

Rose takes the floor in her role as Tatiana's rep and opposition leader, "What's your decision, Victor?"

"Central Beldoc needs a bookshop," he says.

The four of us stare at him, flabbergasted. We hadn't been prepared for this. *Is there a catch?*

"What about my half of the project?" Magda asks. "Are you OK'ing it, too?"

"Of course," Victor says.

Rose eyes him with suspicion. "So, you don't mind that one of the co-owners was born in Russia?"

"The birthplace of Lenin," Victor says, his eyes dreamy. "And Trotsky. And—"

"Hush!" Rose barks, just as Igor was opening his mouth to say something.

I believe her order was aimed at Igor as much as at Victor. Rose knows as well as I do that Igor wasn't going to add another revolutionary to Victor's Hall of Fame. Instead, he was going to declare how much he despises the lot of them, having spent his young years in the totalitarian misery they'd plunged Russia into.

"You're not a Communist anymore, remember?" Rose reminds Victor. "You're a Green now. You're supposed to care about climate change, not Lenin."

Victor looks around as if to check if any of his staff witnessed his slip and getting dressed down by Rose.

Fortunately, none of his aides are currently in the room.

"I'm sure *Monsieur le Maire* was going to mention Tolstoy next," I prompt in an attempt to get us out of the imbroglio.

Victor catches my drift. "Yes, and Valentina Tereshkova, the first woman in space, and Georgy Zhukov, the marshal who beat the Nazis and turned the tide of World War II!"

"Them, I admire greatly," Igor says.

"In that case, welcome to Beldoc," Victor mumbles, still rattled by his gaffe and eager to send us on our way.

He hands the signed permits over to Magda and Igor.

We thank him and scurry out the door before he can change his mind.

CHAPTER 21

I'm serving a customer in the bistro corner of the shop, when a striking young woman wanders in. She looks very familiar…

Oh là là, it's Yoona Han!

She takes a few steps toward the counter and addresses Eric, "I was looking for Julie Cavallo. Is she in today?"

"She'll be with you in a moment."

I set my customer's latte and *canelé* on the table and rush toward Yoona. "*Salut!* So nice of you to stop by!"

Is she here to sample my pastries, like she'd promised, or to try and close the deal on one of her paintings?

She shifts from one foot to the other. "Can we speak in private? I won't take long."

I glance at Eric, who whispers that everything is under control, and lead Yoona to the lab.

"I spoke with Leon yesterday," she announces the moment I pull the door shut.

"Did they let you visit him?"

"I wish!" She blows out her cheeks. "We spoke on the phone."

"What did he tell you?"

"Good things about you, that you'd reached out, and that you'll try to help us."

My stomach knots. After my conversation with Gabriel two days ago, my resolve has weakened. Even Eric and Flo believe that by getting Quentin vindicated, we did our job, and the rest is better left to the professionals. With my team inclined to stop investigating the Rapp family murders, I don't see myself doing it alone.

In other words, I've given up.

Yoona clears her throat. "I'm here about a delicate matter."

"Yes?"

"I need to go into Leon's house."

I blink rapidly. "Why?

"To retrieve my money."

"Pardon me?"

She swallows, glances at the door, and lowers her voice. "Sometimes my clients pay in cash, and those payments stay off the books."

"O-okay."

"You see, I couldn't keep that cash in my house because I have a housemate who I don't trust enough. Definitely not as much as I trusted Horace and Leon."

I'm beginning to understand. "So, you stored your undeclared cash at their house instead of yours."

"That's right," she confirms. "I gave Horace my cash and he put it in a box inside a secret closet in his wing. He brought me the amount I needed when I needed it."

"Wow, you trusted him blindly, didn't you?"

"We kept records." She squares her shoulders. "But yes, I trusted him. He would've died for me."

"Maybe he did, if Leon is the killer."

"How can you say that?!" she leans forward, her eyes

THE BLOODTHIRSTY BEE

burning with emotion. "Leon is the gentlest man I ever met. Despite their rivalry on my account, neither of them would've killed the other."

"OK," I say placatingly. "So. You want to break into the house. I'm afraid I can't help you with that."

"I have Horace's spare keys."

I furrow my brow, perplexed. "Then why do you need me?"

"Because I have no idea where that closet is," she says. "Horace was going to show me, but then he…"

"Died."

She looks away.

"Isn't the house sealed or something?" I ask.

"Not anymore. The gendarmes are done searching it."

"Then maybe they found your money."

"I don't think so," she says. "They would've asked Leon about it. I would've heard."

"Why don't you simply ask Leon where that closet is?"

"He doesn't know about my cash or about Horace's hiding place."

"Still, if you need your money badly enough, you could ask him for an educated guess."

"Don't you think I've tormented him enough already?"

I screw up my face. "I… guess so."

"And now he's in prison, borderline depressed." She takes her head in her hands. "Revealing at this point that I'd entrusted my secret to Horace, and not to him, may just push him over the edge."

She isn't entirely wrong there.

"But why come to me for help?" I ask. "Don't you have a sibling or a trusted friend to help you search for your money?"

"Your sleuthing expertise is one reason."

"Ah, I see my reputation has reached Pont-de-Pré!"

"We have an acquaintance in common," she says. "She's one of my biggest fans and most regular customers."

"Who?"

"Baroness Charlotte Cordes D'Auzon."

Around this time last year, FERJ solved a case involving the young baroness. It was almost as messy and inscrutable as this one. We had the power to ruin her future by revealing her shocking arrangement to the world or by sharing it with the investigators. But we chose not to because it was unrelated to the murder at hand. We simply went ahead and forgot what we'd learned about her.

During the same memorable case, I chose to forget an explosive truth I'd learned about Vero's bestie Sophia. I never regretted that decision.

"Charlotte told me that your detecting savvy is only matched by your discretion," Yoona says. "And that's my second reason for coming to you for help."

I stare at her, unsure how to react, undecided about what to do.

"Will you help me?" she asks, holding my gaze. "Will you come with me to Leon's house?"

"When?"

Wait, what? Did I just make up my mind? Is my pathological curiosity making me throw caution to the wind once again? For all I know, the charming Yoona who needs my help could be in league with the murderer .

"Tonight, after dark," she says. "If you're free."

My mouth opens by itself, and my tongue moves of its own accord. "Tonight it is then."

CHAPTER 22

At eight I send Flo home to Tino. After I lock up the shop and roll down the security curtain, I head to the corner where Yoona is waiting for me in her royal green Mini Cooper.

We drive to Pont-de-Pré in silence.

I steal a look at her.

She can't be the murderer, can she? So delicate, so artistic. Anyway, what would be her motive unless she's a psychopath? If that is the case, then it's good I have my self-defense pocketknife that I always carry around in my purse since last November.

Yoona parks her car in the garage at her place, and we walk to Leon's house.

Checking that there's no one around, Yoona opens the door to Horace's screened wing. I'm half expecting an alarm to go off, but the house is eerily silent. We step in, and pull the door shut as quietly as possible.

The shutters are closed everywhere, but we don't flick on any switches. We use the flashlights we brought with us instead.

"Ready?" I ask Yoona.

Her chest heaves. "Let's do this."

For the next hour and a half, we open every door, move every piece of furniture, and check underneath and behind it. We comb through Horace's wing, then continue to the central part that used to be Coralie's, and then search Leon's wing, too, just in case.

No secret closets anywhere, no matter how freely one interprets the term *closet*. In this instance, we apply the broadest possible interpretation and check every wardrobe, kitchen cabinet, and drawer in the house. There are no boxes with Yoona's cash. Loosening our interpretation further still, we lift every carpet and rug to find smooth floorboards underneath. No banknotes.

It's almost midnight.

Yoona and I sit down on the living room sofa, exhausted, and stare at the wall. Not the wall itself, but at the floor-to-ceiling wall-to-wall library that hides it from view.

Hmm... It was behind a bookshelf that Gustave and Charlotte Cordes d'Auzon hid their secret boudoir.

My energy resurging, I bolt to the library. Fingers interlaced behind my back, I move from one end of it to the other, looking at the books. Nothing mismatched, no volumes placed upside down. After the visual scan, Yoona and I start pulling out books at random, left and right, high and low, hoping to discover a closet door behind. But the wall is smooth, and the shelves are bolted to it, immovable.

Merde, alors!

"It isn't here," Yoona says, sliding down to the floor.

I lower myself next to her. "What are we missing?"

"Nothing." She hangs her head between her knees. "I give up."

"Are you sure?"

"Yeah."

"And your cash?"

"Maybe it's gone," she murmurs. "Maybe a gendarme found it during the search and pocketed it without telling anyone. Maybe it's a sign I should've declared it."

I flash my teeth. "Easy come, easy go is a common fate of ill-gotten gains."

"Very apropos."

"Isn't it?"

Yoona leans back on the bookcase and stretches out her legs. "I just need another minute to rest, and I'll drive you home."

This is as good a time as any to ask her a question that's been bugging me. "Who did you prefer, Horace or Leon?"

"If I had an answer to that question, I would've married that brother months ago, instead of shuttling between them, unable to choose."

"But they were so different!"

"And therein lies the rub," she says. "Horace and I could almost read each other's mind because we were so alike—worldly, shrewd, true go-getters."

"And Leon?"

"Leon is a dreamer. A beautiful, pure soul." She lifts her head and gives me a pensive look. "He is who I wish I were."

As her femme fatale image wavers in my mind, she adds, "Many here think I'm a heartless bitch. Coralie did."

"You don't know that."

"Oh, but I do! I've had reports."

"From who?"

"Townsfolk, random well-wishers... And you know what? I don't blame her." She cradles her head in her hands. "Trust me, that love triangle was as much a curse for me as it was for Horace and Leon."

We fall silent.

I stare at the polished boards we're sitting on. It's the

same oak parquet sprinkled with rugs here and there as in every room of Horace's wing. That is, except for the tiled kitchen and restrooms. Oh, in his home office, the covering is a fitted wall-to-wall carpet. That's the only carpet we didn't try to lift, assuming it was glued or riveted to the floor.

"Let me check just one more thing," I say, heaving myself up.

Once in Horace's office, I squat and attempt to pry off the nearest corner of the carpet. It is as well fixed to the floor as it looked. And because I made the effort to drag myself back into this room, I trudge to the opposite corner, move an armchair, and slip my fingertips under the carpet. To my surprise, I meet no obstacles. I grip the edge and lift. No resistance. Backing on my knees, I peel off more of it and discover a trap door underneath.

"Over here!" I call to Yoona.

She scrambles into the room and kneels beside me. "Holy cow!"

The door is handleless with a keypad embedded into it.

"Any idea what the code may be?" I ask Yoona.

She gives me a coy smile. "Let's try my birthday."

I key it in. Nothing happens. We try Horace's birthday, with the same lack of success.

"Maybe it's his late mother's or aunt's birthday or a random combination," I suggest. "We can draw up a list tomorrow."

Yoona chews at her bottom lip. "Let's try one more thing."

She dictates a six-digit combination that I put in. And, lo and behold, something clicks inside the mechanism, and the door slides open.

"It's the day of my first vernissage in Pont-de-Pré," she explains, looking at me. "Horace and I met on that day."

We shine our flashlights into the opening. I make out a wooden ladder. Without giving it a second thought, I climb down the narrow steps. When my feet reach the hard floor, it occurs to me that, if Yoona is behind it all, then this can be a ruse to trap me in the cellar.

How could I be so reckless?

Half-expecting to hear the click of the door locking over my head, I stand still and let my eyes adjust.

There's a hint of dampness in the air and a relatively strong smell of paint, but the space is definitely ventilated. I touch the wall. It must've been painted at least a week ago, maybe more, because it feels completely dry.

I find a light switch. A bulb hanging from a cord flickers on. Horace's "closet" is a small cellar that's been converted into a room. The conversion is very recent, judging by the smell of paint, and by how spotless everything is.

Yoona grabs either side of the ladder and comes down. *Phew.*

I study the room. It has a small desk, two folding chairs, a cot, some shelves with books and disks, and a pantry with canned food. In one corner, packs of 1.5-liter bottles of Evian are stacked neatly in a tower.

"Looks like a bomb shelter..." I turn to Yoona. "Was Horace a survivalist?"

"If he was, he never told me about it," she says while exploring the room.

I notice a monitor on one of the shelves. Next to it, sits a flat plastic box that resembles a DVD player or a modem.

Can this be some kind of home CCTV system? Does that mean there are hidden cameras in the house? *Has our intrusion been filmed?* That said, I'm planning to go to the gendarmes with all of this, so it doesn't really matter.

"Maybe this was a panic room slash home security station," I muse, pointing to the monitor.

Yoona halts midstride. "He did mention once that he was going to reinforce the entrances and make some adjustments to the house to make it more secure."

"Did he say why? Had the house been burglarized?"

"I don't think so."

An idea begins to form in my mind. "Did he tell you about securing the house while Coralie was still alive?"

"I'm not sure..." She shoots me an apologetic look. "What are you thinking?"

"It may sound far-fetched, but let's assume that before she retired, Coralie had been paid hush money to keep her mouth shut about some dirt."

Yoona blinks. "What kind of dirt?"

"My guess is tax evasion or maybe an affair. Something that her boss didn't want to be known."

Yoona's eyes widen with comprehension. "I always wondered how a retired PA could afford such a major house makeover. She more than tripled the square footage!"

"Did you ever ask Horace or Leon?"

"I did," she replies. "Leon told me he wondered the same thing."

"And Horace?"

"Horace's answer was that Coralie had been a good little squirrel, hoarding money month after month all her life."

This reminds me of how, during our call, Leon used the first person singular and not plural when talking about his suspicions about his aunt's wealth. It was "I" and not "we" who had been asking Coralie questions. It was "I" and not "Horace and I" with the theories she denied. Isn't it strange that the hard-nosed, down-to-earth Horace had been so uncurious about his aunt's unexplained money?

Yoona eyes me intently. "Are you suggesting that Horace knew about Coralie's arrangements and feared they might get her—all of them—in trouble?"

Smart girl! "Something like that."

She claps her hand to her mouth. "Oh my God!"

"What?"

"What if, after Coralie's death, Horace decided to blackmail her former boss?" She wrings her hands. "Wouldn't that explain why he converted this cellar into a panic room?"

I push her hypothesis to its logical culmination, "What if he went through with his plan, and that's what got him killed?"

We stand in the middle of the room, staring at each other in dead silence.

"We should share this theory with the investigators," Yoona finally says. "It may help Leon."

"Agreed."

She fidgets with her ring. "Are you going to tell them why we came here?"

"It won't be necessary."

She draws back, surprised.

"I'm the local amateur sleuth, remember?" I lift a single eyebrow. "I'm the busybody who spied on Horace and took pictures of his killer."

She smiles as her shoulders sag with relief.

Demonstratively, I flip back a strand of hair. "I am Julie Cavallo! I don't need a reason to revisit the crime scene and come up with a new theory."

Yoona's smile becomes sheepish. "Well, since we're here, shall we look for my cash before you send in the cavalry?"

We proceed to examine every shelf and every cabinet. Yoona finds a box with a handful of heirloom jewels. They're lovely. But the gold is thin, and the rocks are on the small side, not the kind to kill for.

"These must be Horace's half of his mom's jewelry,"

Yoona says. "When she was dying, she told him and Leon it was for their future brides."

"Little did she know they'd pick the same woman!"

Yoona doesn't seem to find it funny.

I realize how tactless my comment is and press my palms together. "I'm so sorry!"

"It's the sad truth," she breathes out.

In one of the cabinets, I find another box. This one contains three thick wads of banknotes and a sheet of paper with a hand-drawn table of deposits and withdrawals.

"Oh my God! We found it!" Yoona claps her hands before pulling an identical sheet from her purse. "See? We each had a copy to make sure there are no mistakes or misunderstandings so that this thing doesn't come between us."

She sticks the wads and Horace's sheet into her purse, revealing a small key that lay underneath the money. Its size and shape suggest it isn't a door key or a mailbox key. It looks more like an expensive padlock key, small but sturdy and toothy.

"What does it unlock?" I ask Yoona.

"No idea. It isn't mine."

"I didn't see any padlocks in the house. Did you?"

She shakes her head. "Not one."

On impulse, I pocket the key.

She hikes a beautiful eyebrow. "Did you just swipe a piece of evidence?"

"I… er… borrowed it."

"Ah, that's what it was!" She pulls a falsely self-deprecating face. "How could I not see the difference?"

"I just want to ask Leon about it first. And perhaps make a copy, for my own investigation. But I promise I'll turn it in!"

She giggles. "Take it easy, girl! I'm in no position to moralize."

We leave the house soon after that, agreeing that we'll cooperate fully with the gendarmes about tonight's adventure, but without mentioning Yoona's cash. Or the key I "borrowed."

CHAPTER 23

I called Sophia with my scoop about Horace's cellar first thing in the morning, even before I brought FERJ up to speed. Just as I suspected, the gendarmes that had searched the Rapp brothers' house the first time around had been less thorough than Yoona and me. They hadn't sniffed out the cellar or the nanny cams. They probably hadn't tried too hard, either, after finding the EpiPen in the trash. Why would they? The evidence to indict a suspected killer had been secured, and the goal of the search thus achieved.

At nine-thirty, I heard back from Sophia. She'd briefed Capitaine Loubardin, and he got a warrant for a new search. Sophia and I will meet up tonight for an update and to hand over Horace's key that I'd "borrowed."

In the meantime, I took a photo and sent it to Yoona in case she gets a chance to show it to Leon. I also had a copy made, just in case.

It's six in the evening now. Eric finished his shift and went home. Flo took over behind the counter. I'm in the front shop, giving her a hand. Every customer-free minute we get, we brainstorm the case.

"That pharma company, SivryMed, sounds suspicious as hell," Flo says. "I bet they're involved in both Coralie's and Horace's deaths."

"I think so too, but I can't prove it."

"Would you like me to do a bit of surveillance on Coralie's former boss?"

I shake my head. "It's too dangerous. These people aren't just filthy rich like the Ponsards. They're also well connected. Besides, Ines Kabbaj probably has security guards and cameras all around her house."

"How do we try to get more info then?"

"Indirectly."

She cocks her head. "Meaning?"

"By paying a visit to SivryMed and talking to Coralie's former colleagues."

"Under what pretext? Why would they agree to talk to us? Why would they even let us enter the premises?"

Out of ideas, I scratch my head.

She raises a finger. "Now, if we could fast-forward two years to when I'm a regular contributor to art magazines with proper journalistic credentials and a press card, I could say I was working on a story about the Rapp family curse."

"Marie-Jo!"

Flo jumps at my outburst. "You mean Marie-Jo Barral, Grandma's crony?"

"And editor in chief of *Beldoc Live*! Why didn't I think of her earlier?"

I grab my phone and find Marie-Jo's number.

Having heard me out, she asks, "What's in it for me? We already printed a story about Horace Rapp."

"And what a boring story it was! But now you can have a

gripping one, looking into a Beldoc area family that rivals the Kennedys for a drama-per-person ratio."

"Yeah, right, the Kennedys!"

"Think about it," I press on. "One possible murder, one certain murder, and many, many unanswered questions."

"Who will write the story?"

"Me, obviously."

"Have you written such pieces before?"

I'm forced to admit that no, I haven't.

"I don't question your detective skills, but writing an exciting piece about a case isn't the same as investigating it."

"Give me a chance!" I plead.

"Have you written anything before that's been printed?"

"Do menus count?"

"No."

As I brace myself for a "Sorry, but I can't help you," Marie-Jo surprises me by exclaiming, "This could work, actually!"

"Could it?"

"I'll arrange for the interviews. You'll go with Noam."

I take a moment to process her announcement. Noam Toche is her best investigative journalist. He's all right, I guess, but our relationship has been strained ever since his biased coverage of Brice Dol's case. The article he'd written about Brice's murder was basically a *j'accuse* pointing at Eric. True, he later ate humble pie and apologized profusely, but I haven't quite forgiven him yet.

"Those are my terms," Marie-Jo says. "You'll go as Noam's assistant. He'll conduct the interviews and then he'll write the piece."

"But I have questions—"

"You'll get a chance to slip them in," she says. "Sparingly."

Left with no choice, I agree.

She says she'll be in touch.

Shortly after we hang up, Yoona calls to tell me she had Leon on the phone, and he has no clue what the little key we found could be for. *Merde!*

At eight, we lock up, Flo goes home, and I wait for my cab.

It arrives right on time. I hop in. The driver is a middle-aged man in a nondescript shirt and blue jeans. On his face, however, he's sporting an audacious Salvador Dali mustache that makes me think of Igor. Men—especially older men and certain gendarmes that shall not be named—tend to be conservative about their clothes and coiffure. Styling their facial hair is as much about saying "Look how virile I am" as it is about permitting a glimpse of their personality.

"To Bellegarde, right, Madame?" the driver asks.

"Yes, please. Do you know the *crêperie* across from the town hall?"

He does. Twenty minutes later, I enter the funky restaurant that serves some of the best crêpes and savory buckwheat galettes in Bouches-du-Rhône. Sophia is already there.

We order our drinks and crêpes.

"I'm guessing you can't wait to find out if Horace's home CCTV yielded anything useful," she says.

"You bet!" I zero in on my plate before adding, "But I don't want you to break any rules and get in trouble over leaking information."

"You'll keep your mouth shut, won't you?"

"I will." I glance at her askance. Putting her in this situation is killing me.

"Julie, I owe you big time," she says. "So, stop fretting. Anything I can do for you makes me feel better."

"I've been helpful to your and Loubardin's investigation,

haven't I? First, I got you pix of the blond guy with the beehive and then the tip about the cellar."

She smiles. We both know that's not what she meant, and not why she feels she owes me. But we've never spoken about it. And, as far as I am concerned, I have no intention of doing so, ever.

"You saved my ass," she says.

In response, I blow out a noisy breath. "*Ma belle,* I get all the melodrama I can handle from *Fazenda Passions.* Please, save it for a less saturated recipient."

She chuckles at that.

Satisfied, I add, "I won't say no to an update, though."

"The CCTV footage goes back only two weeks," she says. "It's how those systems work. Programmed deletion to free up space in the cloud for newer footage."

"Did anything suspicious happen during the two weeks prior to Horace's murder?"

"No."

I grimace with disappointment.

"But something did happen after his death," she says, smiling enigmatically.

I lean so far over the table that my breasts are practically in my galette.

"On the night after Leon's arrest," she says, "someone broke into the house. A professional, from the looks of it."

"What did he look like? What did he do? Was he identified? Who was it?"

"Easy, I'm getting there." She looks around to check nobody's listening. "The intruder was able to pick the lock to get in, and then relock the front door on his way out."

"Is that even possible?"

"With a good pick gun, patience and skill, it is."

I nod. "Go on."

THE BLOODTHIRSTY BEE

"He was of slight built, not very tall. He wore a face mask, a cap, and gloves."

"What did he steal?"

"He opened every drawer and cabinet, every binder in the office, every jar and cookie tin in the kitchen," she says. "He was looking for cash, but also for documents."

"He was sent there by Coralie's former boss at SivryMed, I'm sure!"

"Capitaine Loubardin isn't a big fan of that new theory of yours."

"Why not?" I sit back, frowning. "Can't he see how much sense it makes?"

"He believes you're letting your preconceived ideas cloud your judgment."

I launch a theatrical eye roll when a bulb goes off in my head. "Skinny and shortish, you said, right? So is Leon, except he was already in police custody. And you know who else had the same build and height?"

"The blond man that killed Horace."

I gesture at her with an open palm. "Exactly! The man we thought was Leon. But what if it was a hitman hired by Ines Kabbaj's to kill Horace and frame Leon?"

"We can't rule that out."

"She then sent same guy into the Rapp house to look for any dossiers that Coralie may have had on her."

"It's a theory worth exploring, if you ask me," Sophia says.

"If only he didn't wear a mask and a cap! If only we could see his face and ID him!"

She grins. "We did."

"What do you mean?"

"At one point, he was too warm from all the crawling around and moving furniture to check behind it," she says.

"His breathing became pained. So, he removed the mask for a minute."

She falls silent.

All my muscles taut, I wait for the big reveal.

But Sophia is in no rush.

"This is torture," I lament. "How can you do this to me?"

"Fine, fine! We identified the intruder as one Regis Chouquet."

"So, he was already in your database! A professional?"

"A legend among burglars, released from jail only a few weeks ago." Sophia looks around again. "It is whispered that no lock in the known universe can resist him."

"Wow, impressive!"

"Yeah, he rocks at breaking in." She winks at me. "But less so at not getting caught. Three prison sentences under his belt already."

"Three? Did he start as a child?"

"None of his priors involved violence," she says. "And with how clement our system is, he never stayed in prison long."

I contort my upper lip. "The system wasn't so clement when it imprisoned an innocent man for a year!"

"You mean your buddy Quentin Vernet? The ME on that case was sanctioned. He should've flagged the Nardil in his report and correlated it with the higher-than-normal level of caffeine."

"Was Commissaire Anjara punished, too?" I ask. "It was his fixation on chiropractic adjustments and his gut feeling that Quentin was guilty that may have influenced the ME to interpret the data a certain way."

"Commissaire Anjara received a reprimand."

"Good!" I join my hands at my chest. "May I share that part with Quentin? He'd be so pleased to hear it!"

"Yes, you may."

"OK, back to our burglar, Chouquet," I say. "Was he alone?"

"Yes. If he had an accomplice, then that person stayed outside as the lookout and didn't get caught on tape."

"Do you think someone hired Chouquet to look for something?" I ask. "Or maybe he just heard the house was empty and tried his luck?"

"At this point, we can't tell if the break-in was premeditated or opportunistic."

A detail from the morning Horace was killed flashes in my mind. "Is Regis Chouquet blond?"

"No, he isn't. Not in his natural state, at any rate."

"He could've been wearing a blond wig that day, to make sure that if a witness saw him, the description would match Leon." I clap a hand to my forehead. "That explains the absence of a cap!"

"You believe it was too careless not to be intentional?"

"I do, yes."

She studies my face. "I'm sensing you're as convinced now of Leon Rapp's innocence as you were of Quentin Vernet's."

"And I was right about Quentin, wasn't I?"

"It appears so."

I push my chest out, pleased with her admission. "Did Chouquet find anything in the house?"

"A bit of cash in a desk drawer."

"No documents?"

She shakes her head. "Mind you, there are no cameras in Leon's wing, so we're not clear if he found something in there."

"Have you arrested him yet?"

"We're working on it."

I give her a quizzical look.

"He wasn't at his last known address," she says. "We've put out a BOLO."

"I hope you find him soon, question him, and establish he was doing Ines Kabbaj's dirty work!"

We finish our meal and pay. Sophia must get back to her teenage kids, and I, to my soap opera, since Gabriel is away and I'm too tired to bicycle over to Rose's.

"Whatever you do next, please be careful," Sophia tells me as we head to her car. "Those pharma bosses are some of the richest and most powerful people in the world these days."

"More powerful than the judge I exposed last fall?"

She ignores my question. "You were lucky to survive last fall, playing with fire like you did! Need I remind you how close you came to being murdered?"

"You needn't," I say, climbing into the passenger seat. "I have Rose and also Gabriel to remind me every chance they get."

Perhaps I should listen, shouldn't I?

CHAPTER 24

Noam and I pass through the security gates and enter the SivryMed premises.

A hostess leads us upstairs. Even though we're in the administrative wing, far from the chemical heart of the company, there's no mistaking what SivryMed's core business is. This place is the antithesis of Beldoc's town hall. Everything here is modern and new. No wood, but lots of metal, glass, and plastic—all of it smooth and shiny. Even the potted jade plants enlivening the aisles are so unnaturally green they look like they were embalmed in formaldehyde.

Black screens glowing blue punctuate the gleaming white workstations. The smell of hand sanitizer is so pervasive it dominates all other smells, including the ladies' flowery perfumes and gentlemen's lemony colognes.

The bottom half of the walls is lined with locked glass cabinets holding sophisticated equipment, test tubes, and vials. The upper half is decorated with framed posters. In the bright electrical light, I observe the stylish renditions of medicinal plants, the periodic table of elements, and close-ups of ecstatic citizens as they enjoy the benefits of the company's newest pill or injectable.

We advance through a vast open-space office. It's as freakily sleek as the rest of it. But at least the background sounds here are what you'd expect from a workplace full of humans. Swivel chairs slide across the floor, printers whir, phones beep softly, and staffers answer them or talk to each other in hushed tones.

The hostess leads us into a break room with couches and coffee machines. Two middle-aged women nursing mugs in their hands are waiting there for us. They must be Nadine Tupinier and Mireille Cuisance—two of Coralie's former colleagues that agreed to answer our questions.

With the introductions made, the hostess leaves. Noam turns on his recorder, and I open my notebook.

"What was Coralie like?" he asks the ladies.

"Outgoing, always ready to help, smart, extremely entertaining," Mireille says.

Nadine's eyes crinkle up. "While all of that is true, she did have a mean streak in her."

Noam turns to her. "Can you give us an example?"

"It's hard to recall a specific instance..." Nadine glances at Mireille. "Let's just say, she wasn't tender, even with the people she was helping out. She could ridicule and trash you, and rub your nose in your uselessness, until you regretted asking her for help."

Mireille nods. "Take her nephews. She adored them, lived and breathed for them, but she lambasted almost every life choice and decision they made."

"Like, for example, when Leon decided to open a dog grooming salon," Nadine adds. "She thought it was a terrible idea."

Mireille cups her cheeks. "Oh là là, we never heard the

THE BLOODTHIRSTY BEE

end of it, even when he was three years into his business and making a profit!"

"Did she ever mention Yoona Han?" I ask.

The ladies exchange a meaningful look.

"That woman moved into Pont-de-Pré and bewitched Horace and Leon after Coralie had retired." Nadine flashes a sly grin. "But, yes, we did hear about her."

"Whenever Coralie would come by to have lunch with us, she spent half of the time hating on the heartless bitch," Mireille says.

Heartless bitch. I've heard those exact words already—from Yoona herself.

"Coralie once confronted that Yoona woman," Nadine says. "She told her to stop torturing her boys and find herself a new victim. And you know what the witch said to that?"

"Tell us," Noam says.

It's Mireille who does. "Yoona had the gall to tell Coralie that her feelings for Leon and Horace were genuine, that she was in love with both of them. Can you believe it?"

"Those poor boys!" Nadine rubs the area above her D cups. "Fatherless, mother dies in their teens, Leon grows up to be more comfortable around dogs than humans, Horace has several allergies, one of which deadly—"

I start at the last item on her list of woes. "You knew about Horace's bee venom allergy?"

Both women nod.

"Coralie told us long ago," Nadine says. "Horace had been stung once before. He developed a severe reaction, was taken to the ER, and administered some lifesaving drug. I don't recall the name now…"

"Epinephrine," Noam says.

"That's the one!" Nadine sits back, satisfied. "The doctors had told him to avoid getting stung again. He was to never leave the house without his EpiPen because a second sting could be worse."

Hmm, would it be too wild to assume that Coralie had also shared these tidbits with Ines?

"Were Coralie and Ines close?" I ask.

"Oh yes, very," both women confirm.

"Did Coralie ever criticize her, or her decisions?" Noam asks. "Be it to her face, or behind her back?"

Once again, the women exchange a look, only this time neither of them volunteers an answer.

"Given the way you described her personality," I say, rushing to Noam's rescue, "there must've been things going on in the company that Coralie disapproved of."

Silence.

I look from Nadine to Mireille. "No monkey business? Irregular shenanigans? Come on!"

The pair of them look so ill at ease and almost scared that I fear they're going to beat a retreat.

But before they can make a run for it, the door opens, and a fit, well-dressed woman enters the room. In her forties, she has the same kind of long, shiny black hair as Yoona. Only hers is pulled back into a severe bun.

She marches straight up to Noam. "Ines Kabbaj, head of R&D. I was Coralie's boss for seven years, from the day she joined us until the day she retired."

"I'm so happy you were able to make time for this interview, Madame!" Noam points at me. "This is Julie, my assistant."

Ines gives me a tiny nod without bothering to shift her eyes from him. "What exactly do you hope to learn about Coralie, Monsieur Toche? What kind of article are you writing?"

"It's going to be a story about her and her nephews," he

explains. "How fate seems to be determined to annihilate them all."

I motion Ines to a vacant chair. "Please."

She sits down.

"Readers love family-curse stories, and this is the most memorable we've had in the Arles region for a while," Noam says.

Ines makes a skeptical *hmm*.

To help put her more at ease, I ask, "Was Coralie easy to work with? Was she good at her job?"

"The best!" She perks up. "I've gone through three PAs since she retired, and not one of them can compare. Coralie was highly competent, remarkably efficient, and at the same time attentive to detail and meticulous."

"That's a rare beast," I say.

"A unicorn!" Ines smiles. "The downside is, she ruined all other PAs for me, even the objectively good ones."

Mireille and Nadine give a polite chuckle.

"Do you think Leon Rapp murdered his aunt Coralie, and then his brother Horace?" I ask Ines.

She spreads her hands. "Frankly, I don't know what to think."

The door opens again. This time, it's a man in his early fifties. He has that unique clout, that air of dominance about him that only people invested with real power give off. Well, and perhaps a few gifted actors that manage to mimic it.

All three employees rise to their feet. Instinctively, Noam and I do the same.

"Paul Sivry, CEO of SivryMed," he announces, gesturing for everyone to sit down.

Wow, the big boss himself! Paul Sivry carved a moment in his busy schedule to attend an interview by a local paper about a former secretary at his firm. *Not unusual at all.*

After Noam and I introduce ourselves, he addresses

Noam, "What exactly is the nature of the piece you're writing?"

Is it me, or is the SivryMed management a tad on edge?

"Since you're here, and since you probably won't stay long," Noam says in a suddenly different, more solemn, tone, "I'm going to go ahead and ask the question I was saving for last."

Paul Sivry's eyes crinkle to slits. "Shoot."

"Was Coralie a whistle-blower?" Noam's expression is hard. "Was she openly critical of your latest drug, SivryPack?"

Paul's face is now as hard as Noam's. The break room is so silent you can hear the printer next door as the two men launch a staring contest.

"SivryPack passed the trial phase with flying colors and was approved for sale," Noam says. "And then nasty adverse effects started cropping up left and right. You haven't withdrawn it yet, but you're facing many lawsuits. Would you like to comment on that?"

As Noam speaks, I gawk at him, flabbergasted. It isn't for nothing, after all, that Marie-Jo considers him her best reporter!

The tension in the room becomes palpable.

While everyone looks expectantly at Paul, I can't help admiring Noam. The man did his homework. He came to this interview armed with concrete, specific knowledge. While I suspected that something fishy may be going on here, I hadn't really followed up on my hunch. Flo hadn't probed into the company beyond a quick internet search. Except, quick searches are tricky.

They become downright useless when you're investigating people with means. They all hire cleaners to curate their online rep. Favorable content gets bumped to the top of the search, while the rest is spammed to bury the negative stories so deep no one will find them. The practice isn't even reserved to the rich and mighty anymore. It's gone mainstream. Heck, my little shop received an unsolicited quote from my bank for a service package that included pushing our positive reviews up and the negative ones down!

I confess I was tempted. What business doesn't dream of seeing the negative feedback, often posted by competitors, go away?

Paul Sivry stands up sharply. "This interview is over."

His employees jump to their feet.

Ines opens the door and hollers. "Over here!"

Two massive security guards hurtle into the room.

"Please see these reporters out," Paul orders, heading for the exit. Ines bolts behind him. Mireille and Nadine scurry after them.

The guards escort Noam and me out of the building.

Once on the street, I put a hand to my heart. "Bravo! What you did there was so cool! I forgive you for going after Eric two years ago."

"I'm glad to hear it," Noam says. "It's a shame, though, that the SivryMed bosses kicked us out before we could get any answers."

"The way they reacted was an answer in itself, don't you think?"

He inclines his head. "I'll keep digging. And I'll write a story Paul Sivry won't like."

"Will you let me know if you uncover anything that could shed light on the Bray-Rapp case?" I ask him.

"You can count on it," he promises before we part ways.

CHAPTER 25

I get back to the shop, and immediately clue in Eric. A little later, I call Rose, and when Flo arrives to take over from Eric, I update her, too, between customers. Thursday afternoons are busy times, so the minutes and hours fly by until it's eight.

When Flo and I close the shop, Noam is waiting outside in Karl's favorite spot under the oak tree.

"What did you do to my friends?" I ask him jokingly.

He gives me a blank stare.

"Karl and his dog, Harley," I clarify. "They often hang out here around closing time."

Noam raises his chin slowly. "Ah. The hobo. He wasn't here when I arrived."

"Julie told me about your bombshell question at SivryMed," Flo tells him. "Well done!"

Instead of looking pleased, Noam's face contorts with anger. "Marie-Jo is shelving my story."

"What?" Flo and I ask at once.

"She received a call from high up with an ultimatum."

"Who called her?" I draw closer. "Paul Sivry?"

"No."

"Our mayor?" Flo asks.

"Aim higher."

"The mayor of Arles?"

He smirks. "Higher still."

"An MP? A senator? A prefect? A minister?"

He releases a sigh. "Let's just say it was a person who has the power to cut the public subsidies to *Beldoc Live*."

"Argh!" Flo balls her hands into fists. "I hate the way this world works!"

"I'm so gutted I'm thinking about resigning from *Beldoc Live*," Noam says.

I touch his arm. "Please don't make rash decisions! Marie-Jo thinks the world of you. If she dropped your story, it means she had no choice."

"I know, I know." He waves us goodbye. "Don't worry, I won't quit tonight. I'll take a long walk and sleep on it."

After he leaves, Flo heads to the bus stop.

I straddle my bike to ride to Rose's for a slice of quiche and an episode of *Fazenda Passions*, when a phone call diverts me.

It's Quentin asking if I have any news.

"And on your end?" I counter.

I don't really expect him to have any new information, but one can always hope. Besides, I need a minute to calm my emotions after Noam's upsetting news. I wouldn't want to inadvertently betray Sophia's trust and reveal something to Quentin that I shouldn't.

"I keep bugging Anjara," he says. "The good commissaire keeps telling me he and his team are on it, but they haven't made any headway yet."

I tell Quentin about this morning's visit to SivryMed. With Noam's article dead in the water, not only do I have no reason to keep it a secret from

Quentin, but I feel like shouting about it to the whole world.

"It's a shame your reporter friend pulled the heavy artillery too soon," Quentin comments when I'm done.

"What do you mean?"

"He should've let you do the talking," he says. "With your friendly manner and seemingly innocent questions, you may've gotten something out of those two employees..."

"Mireille and Nadine."

"Yes, Mireille and Nadine."

"They were too scared to talk," I say. "Or maybe they sincerely saw no evil."

"Yeah, right."

"Why the sarcasm?" I tease him. "Don't you believe that Paul Sivry is an honest actor, working tirelessly for the good of humanity? That his goal is to help sick people get better, and not help himself get richer?"

Quentin laughs a bitter laugh. "If I believed that, I'd also believe that modern medicine wants to cure people."

I feign shock. "It doesn't?"

"No, silly. It wants to keep people alive and always sick with one thing or another. There's no money in good health."

I can't help but agree with his cynical remark. "Take what you do, for comparison. You fix people without giving them adverse effects."

"I'm glad you noticed." A note of satisfaction crawls into his lingering resentment.

Pleased that he's pleased, I add, "Isn't it sad that doctors prescribe drugs more readily than a better diet and more exercise?"

"Isn't it sad," he echoes me, "that doctors prescribe drugs for afflictions that could be treated without, knowing full well that every drug is as much a remedy as it is a poison?"

"Especially if you overdose."

"True," he agrees. "Take, for example, the Nardil that killed Coralie. Whether it's medicine or poison is a matter of dosage."

"That's my understanding, too."

"Listen," he says, "I don't want to get carried away. Even if the SivryMed management reeks of guilt, do you think the murders could still be Leon's work?"

"No."

"I trust your instincts, but it's a shame you haven't uncovered any new material evidence."

"Who says I haven't?" *Oops!*

"Do tell!"

Seriously, Julie, couldn't you hold your tongue? "I'm afraid I can't tell you. I'm sworn to secrecy on that one."

"You're cruel."

"Forgive me, my friend! If it's any consolation, you'll find out in due course."

He says he understands, and he'll arm himself with patience. We hang up.

As I pedal to Rose's, my mood gets darker and darker. I'm upset that Noam's story won't be published. I'm annoyed at myself for bragging and teasing Quentin unnecessarily. It bothers me that I swiped the key from Horace's panic room and had to face some unpleasantness when I handed the original to the gendarmes, for nothing.

It also upsets me that Regis Chouquet hasn't been found yet. The longer he stays hidden, the slimmer the chance of locating him and getting something out of him. The official investigation is going nowhere. FERJ's investigation is bumping into brick walls. Leon is still in prison. Quentin hasn't been properly acquitted yet. And the actual villains carry on with their bad deeds, unhindered.

It's in that grim state of mind that I arrive at Rose's and

park the bike by the wall. As I let myself in, the first thing I see is blood on the stairs leading up to the first floor. Not a river or a puddle but still quite a lot. Against the red, prints of Lady's paws show her heading upstairs... and downstairs... and across the stairs, in an erratic pattern.

What happened here?

Is Lady all right? Is Rose all right? Whose blood is this?

"Grandma!" I yell. "Lady!"

"Over here," Rose calls from the ground floor.

I sprint toward her voice.

She's sitting on the floor in the bathroom, holding Lady clumsily while fumbling with a bandage. "Can you help me?"

One of Lady's paws is bleeding.

I sit down next to them.

Rose thrusts Lady into my arms. "Hold her tight so I can bandage the paw."

"What happened?"

"She was running to get her dinner." Rose starts wrapping the white gauze around the paw. "You know how she gets when she smells her food?"

"She goes berserk."

"Exactly!" She checks that the bandage is tight enough to resist Lady's attempts to remove it. "So she was zooming downstairs to the kitchen and broke her nail."

"All that blood on the staircase is from a broken nail?"

Rose looks up at me, scandalized. "Are you saying my baby is faking it? That she dipped her paw in beetroot juice to get attention?"

"She'd never do something so devious, and I'd never assume she might!"

Rose takes Lady from me, hugs her to her chest and kisses the top of her head. "You're the sweetest, purest, prettiest of all my descendants!"

"Including your only great-granddaughter?" I tease her.

Rania, my oldest sister Vero's girl, is usually the one that gets all the superlatives from Rose.

"Even her," Rose says. "No human can compare! Humans are fickle. Their affections don't last. But this canine will never turn her back on me."

What did you smoke this afternoon, Grandma?

Rose covers Lady's head with kisses, tearing up. "You're loyal, *mon amour*. Not like Serge who already found himself a new girlfriend."

Oh, dear.

CHAPTER 26

Strawberry season isn't over yet, but on this Friday morning in mid-May, we're officially closing it within the confines of the pâtisserie.

Before Eric arrived and flipped the sign on the door, I'd changed the window display and the displays inside the shop. Out with the oversized marzipan strawberries and undersized wicker baskets, and in with the calligraphed red lanterns, wafer paper fans, origami cranes, and lacquered chopsticks.

For the rest of the month, we'll be promoting our new line of Japanese-inspired macarons. The featured flavors are matcha green tea, black sesame, and yuzu. We'll also be selling mochi cakes filled with red bean paste and mochi ice cream in two flavors. *Summer is here!*

For the bistro corner menu, I've added iced bubble tea. The manga-gobbling teenagers are the main target for that particular product. More generally, it is my hope that all the Beldocians, and not just the teens who can't afford our top-of-the-range pastries, will love the new line as much as Eric, Flo, and I do.

With the displays redone and Eric manning the counter, I retreat into the kitchen. Just before the lunchtime influx, I step away from my ovens to sip the expresso that Eric brewed for both of us. With the shop momentarily empty, we plant ourselves outside the window and admire the new display from the sidewalk. There's a commotion across the street. Magda and Igor, accompanied by two men who look like contractors, are visiting the newly acquired premises.

Eric raises his paper cup. "Here's to the future bookshop! I hope it will carry sci-fi and comic strips."

"To Lavender Dream!" I touch my cup to Eric's. "I hope Magda will now stop wishing that I wither and die or go belly up."

We drink, watching the goings-on across the shop. I dip one hand in the pocket of my jeans underneath my double-breasted chef's jacket and fidget with the copy of Horace's key.

What a shame neither Yoona nor Leon knew what it may open!

I fish it out and hold it up for Eric. "Any ideas?"

He's seen the key already, and had no clue, so I don't even know why I bother again. I guess I'm that desperate.

Eric lifts his shoulders apologetically. "Judging by the shape and quality, I'd say it's to a small high-security padlock. But beyond that…"

"Do you own any padlocks like that?"

He nods. "I do."

"What do you use them for?"

"I have a good suitcase that doesn't have a number lock." He scratches his cheek, recalling. "Lea's locker at work. My locker at the gym."

I study the key. "A locker, huh? Why would Horace keep something valuable, like maybe proof of corruption at

SivryMed, in a locker? He had an entire secret room protected by a keypad lock in his house for that."

"You said the room was new, right?"

I lift my gaze to Eric. "It sure looked new. And it still reeked of paint."

"Maybe he was going to move the documents there, eventually. Maybe he was waiting for the paint to dry. Paper doesn't like humidity."

"It's possible," I say. "Or maybe he just didn't want to keep all his eggs in one basket."

"That's possible, too."

I pull my phone from the back pocket of my jeans and call Yoona. "Did Horace have a gym subscription?"

"No, but he worked out at home, and sometimes in that new gym where you pay by the hour."

"Would you happen to know if he had a locker there?"

She takes a moment to think about it. "I believe he did. Sometimes he'd pop into the gallery straight from his gym, which is just a few blocks away. He'd be all showered and dressed, and no gym bags over his shoulder."

"So, the gym is in Pont-de-Pré, then."

"Yes. Why?" I can almost hear her brain churn and spit out the solution. "Oh, right! The key! The padlock!"

Eric touches my shoulder. "I can work overtime and help out Flo if you want to go check that gym out."

Thanking him, I say into the phone, "Can you take a break at five?"

"I'll wait for you at the gallery."

∼

I FOLLOW Yoona through the revolving door of the Pont-de-Pré gym. The man at the reception desk asks us to swipe our cards at the turnstile.

THE BLOODTHIRSTY BEE

"We aren't members," Yoona says.

"Is this your first visit?" He plasters a big grin on his face. "You don't need a subscription to be a member. Fill out a form, get a card, and pay only for the time you actually spend at our gym."

"Sounds lovely," she says, glancing at me for help.

She probably thinks I have a special technique up my sleeve. But the truth is, I just play it by ear.

In this instance, we don't know if the gym is aware of Horace's death. Was the padlock on his locker removed? Was the locker emptied out? Was the stuff inside disposed of? On top of that, we haven't the slightest idea which of the many lockers in this gym—quite a few of them reinforced with padlocks—was Horace's. Provided he had an assigned locker. Provided he had one at all.

Bearing the above in mind, my instinct tells me to put my cards on the table.

I point at Yoona. "Madame Han is the fiancée of your member Horace Rapp who passed away three weeks ago."

"My condolences, Madame," the receptionist says to Yoona, adopting an appropriately somber expression.

"We were wondering if Horace's locker is still reserved under his name?" I place the key on the counter. "This is the key to his padlock."

"I'd like to retrieve his stuff," Yoona says.

The receptionist enters a query into his computer. "The locker was paid for the full month of May, so no one has touched it."

"Great," Yoona says.

But the receptionist hesitates. "I understand you're his fiancée, and you have a key, but... Shouldn't it be the next of kin collecting his belongings?"

"His only surviving next of kin is his brother Leon,

currently imprisoned for Horace's murder," I say. "You can check."

Yoona twitches from the harshness of my statement. But it seems to have worked. The receptionist scribbles a number on a Post-it Note without bothering to verify my assertion.

"Locker thirty-nine." He hands the note to Yoona. "I'll let you in. Head all the way to the back until you bump into the lockers."

Thanking him, we pass the turnstiles and cross the colorful lobby. It's one of those fitness centers that double as a trendy leisure club with designer interior, comfy seating, and a café space.

The fitness area has TV screens high on the wall. Treadmills, stationary bikes, and ellipticals face them to keep the cardio crowd entertained. We walk down the narrow aisle, careful not to trip on a treadmill. The people using them multitask by watching TV, listening to music, or reading a book.

No such frivolities are possible in the weight-lifting area we pass next. Here, straining, red-faced men grunt and drip sweat on the safety mats as they practice self-torture by barbells. A glass door separates the individual effort area from the room where a Zumba class is underway. I can't see the students, but I can hear the energetic music and the no less energetic instructor.

And then, suddenly, we're staring at a wall of lockers. We find locker thirty-nine.

"You try," Yoona says, her voice shaky.

My hands equally shaky, I insert the key into the hole at the bottom of the padlock. It goes all the way in! And it turns! And the padlock clicks open!

Inside, there's a gym bag with a towel, sneakers and joggers, and beneath it, a plastic bag. It contains another plastic bag, and another one encased it like Russian dolls. And inside the innermost bag, is a stack of documents. Some of them are letters and memos on SivryMed letterhead. They bear the signatures of Ines Kabbaj and Paul Sivry in blue ink. Others are tables with data. Yet others are computer screen and cellphone screen grabs that were printed out. And, finally, there are copies of two handwritten letters to Ines and Paul, signed by Coralie Bray.

I look up at Yoona. "You knew nothing of this?"

"No," she says, wide-eyed.

"And Leon?"

"Horace kept him out of the loop, I'm certain of it."

"Because of their rivalry over you?"

"That, too." She pinches her lips, doubtful. "But mostly, because Leon wasn't going to sit on this treasure trove that implicates SivryMed in Coralie's death."

"You're right! Not when he knew that Quentin Vernet was wrongfully accused of it."

She hangs her head, no doubt ashamed that the go-getter she was dating wasn't just a worldly man, but also a douche.

We pack the documents back into the layers of plastic and retreat at a jog.

CHAPTER 27

I'm glad that yesterday was Saturday, the busiest day of the week at the shop. I used the only breather I got to brief Eric about the treasure in Horace's locker, but other than that, there's been no time to discuss or obsess about the case.

In the evening, I called Quentin. His line was busy, so I left him a message telling him there'd been a breakthrough in the case, and the gendarmes now have evidence to go after Ines Kabbaj and Paul Sivry. I apologized for not giving him more and promised that he'll be the first person I call as soon as Capitaine Loubardin or Commissaire Anjara tell me I'm allowed to talk.

Next, I called Dad. In the fall, he went through a rough patch both at work and at home, with Paulette. He was close to quitting the former and being dumped by the latter. But things straightened themselves out since then. He's in a much better place now. My twin Cat is in an even better place these days. Her business is thriving, and she's been dating someone she's very keen on. I hope to hear more about the guy next time we talk.

I binge-watched my Brazilian *telenovela* for the rest of the evening to unwind.

Then came Sunday morning. I did my laundry and grocery shopping. And now Flo and I are at Rose's, for a lunch of Niçoise salad and asparagus quiche. I brought some cake. Flo came with store-bought lemonade.

We set the table in the garden and sit down. Lady who has a fresh bandage around her paw, settles under the table. This new bandage, much more professionally done and brightened up with little green paw prints is definitely the vet's work.

Rose has forbidden us to talk about Serge or ask any questions about the woman he's seeing now. But we're encouraged to discuss anything FERJ related.

I tell them about my trip to Pont-de-Pré, about Horace's locker and what Yoona and I found inside. After we left the gym, we went to Yoona's place. We surveyed the documents we'd found in the locker and photographed them all. Early Saturday morning, she came by, and we delivered everything to Capitaine Loubardin's office at the Bellegarde Gendarmerie.

"Was he there?" Flo asks.

"No," I say, "And it was a huge relief."

Rose pours me more wine. "Oh, don't worry, he'll give you a call soon enough to tell you that you should've gone to him *before*, and not after opening the locker."

"And if he doesn't," Flo chimes in, "I'm sure Sophia will."

I narrow my eyes at them. "Whose side are you on?"

"The side of law and order," Flo replies.

"Broadly speaking," Rose adds.

In truth, it's hard to disagree with them. And if Sophia doesn't chastise me, then I bet Gabriel will as soon as he gets home on Tuesday. Since he left, we've been exchanging text messages, just to let each other know we're fine. He's part of some big operation over in Marseilles which keeps him busy and constantly on his toes. The one time we squeezed in a video chat, he was obliged to hang up five minutes in and take his boss's call. And then he had to go.

"Back to Horace's stash," Flo says.

I unlock my phone. "We have a photo of every single document—"

"Can you sum up their content, so we don't have to read them?" my lazy sister asks.

"How unprofessional of you," I berate her.

"On the contrary, it's super professional of me!" The cheeky bastard rolls her shoulders. "You spent... how many hours last night studying them?"

"At least three."

She serves herself more salad. "Your summary will therefore save FERJ three person-hours."

"Non-billable person-hours," Rose adds.

I finish my first slice of quiche and explain to them that all the various documents in the locker fall into two big categories. The first one comprises internal memos, database grabs, printouts, and photos. It constitutes strong evidence that SivryMed falsified the results of the trial phase for its latest drug. Ines and Paul were involved in the fraud, as well as a handful of other people including Coralie. The second group consists of the letters Coralie wrote to Ines and Paul, threatening to expose their fraud.

"She wrote the first letter before she retired," I say. "In it, she complains that her hush money was insufficient."

"Do you think they topped it up?" Rose asks.

I nod. "It logically follows from the second letter."

Flo breaks off a piece of baguette and wipes her plate. "What does that one complain about?"

"It's dated a month before she died. She's asking for a

third and final payment to ensure she keeps her mouth shut."

"Your instincts were right about her bosses being fishy," Rose remarks.

"Yes, only where I suspected adultery, tax evasion or embezzlement, the wrongdoing that led to two murders was worse."

"Horace knew about it, didn't he?" Flo reaches for the quiche. "Coralie had confided in him. More than that, she'd entrusted him with the proof of SivryMed's fraud and of her blackmail operation."

"It all makes so much more sense now!" Rose exclaims.

"It really does, doesn't it?" I shift my gaze from my grandma to my sister. "Here's what I think happened next. After Coralie suffered a stroke and died, Horace threw caution to the wind and attempted to blackmail SivryMed in his turn."

"He may have even believed her death had been accidental, caused by Quentin's mistake," Flo lisps with her mouth full.

"It's possible," I say, thinking aloud. "But knowing what he knew about Coralie blackmailing SivryMed, I'm surprised he didn't point an accusatory finger at them."

Rose shrugs a single shoulder. "On the other hand, Commissaire Anjara's investigation had concluded medical malpractice and the ME hadn't raised any red flags, right?"

"Yes," I reply.

"It was so much easier for Horace to accept that as true," Rose says.

"Anjara's version freed Horace from the guilt he might've felt for not dissuading his aunt from her blackmail scheme," Flo adds.

"True," I say. "That neat version also meant Horace

didn't have to ruin Coralie's reputation posthumously. In every way, it was much too convenient to pooh-pooh."

Flo brushes breadcrumbs off her lap. "So. A year passes. Quentin is released. Jobless, he goes to Dubai to try his hand at gardening. Yoona and the Rapp brothers are stuck in their love triangle. Life follows its course."

"And then, a few weeks ago, Horace gets greedy," I narrate in the same tone. "Or maybe he runs into money problems. Or convinces himself he can outsmart everyone."

"Coralie died before she could claw her final payment from SivryMed, yes?" Rose asks.

"That's what I think," I reply. "Horace relaunched the blackmail. He didn't make copies of his own blackmail letter, though."

"That doesn't mean he hadn't written it," Flo says.

"And in response," Rose concludes, "the perverse SivryMed execs hired a hitman that killed Horace and framed his brother Leon."

All three of us take a moment to let that mental movie settle in our minds.

"Do the documents prove Leon didn't kill his brother?" Flo asks.

"No," I say. "But they give the police a new lead and two plausible suspects."

Flo lifts the bottle of her much-too-sweet lemonade. "More? Do you think they'll let Leon out on bail?"

"None for me." I snatch away my glass, just in case.

She rolls her eyes. "Snob."

"Leon's problem," I say, ignoring her taunt, "is that there's material evidence against him."

Flo refills her own glass. "Ah, yes, the EpiPen."

"On the other hand, everything tying Paul Sivry to Horace's and Coralie's deaths is circumstantial."

Rose picks Lady up. "SivryMed will lawyer up. The

investigators will have to double-check everything. They'll need to prove the fraud was real, then prove the blackmail took place, find the money trail, and tie Paul and Ines to the murders."

That's many, many painstaking steps before Quentin and Leon can be vindicated.

"I hope the cops find the burglar, Regis Chouquet!" I cry.

"If they do and if he talks," Flo says, her eyes lighting up, "then Ines and Paul will have a hard time wriggling out of this, despite all their money and connections."

Rose lifts her eyes to the sky. "May the universe hear you and serve Ines and Paul their karma in this lifetime!"

CHAPTER 28

Bookkeeping Monday is upon me. Alone in the shop, I toil away, logging receipts and invoices and reconciling my ledger with the bank statement. As always when I do something I hate, my mind strays oft and far.

Right now, I'm thinking about the tall guy I saw two weeks ago, when catering the Ponsards' party. Was he really the man from my snapshot? Was he the fugitive contractor?

If only I'd snapped a pic before running off to the kitchen to fetch more crumble! Then my sisters and I would have more to work with than Flo's approximative sketch based on my description. We could do a reverse image search. I could get Gabriel or Sophia to run it through the gendarmerie database. We could find that man and make sure that he faced a trial and a verdict—no matter how lax—after all these years for what he'd done.

If he is indeed the beach-house contractor, then he's no doubt using a new alias. Moreover, he must be convinced that the events of that fateful summer are long forgotten. He believes that it's safe for him to be back in Provence, to show his face at crowded events, and to run a business of some kind.

What if he's still a builder? What if his ineptitude kills another person?

Thinking about his nerve and how smug he must be feeling—the clever one that got away with manslaughter—stirs something related in my mind. Something about the current case... Something that's been tucked away for a while now, sending distress signals and being ignored...

What is it? Why do I resent and resist exploring it?

Because I won't like where it may lead me.

That thought is as unexpected as a splutter of oil from a cold skillet. And then, as if an invisible switch is flipped and brings my mind to a boil, a slew of overlooked details and suppressed inferences fizz up to the surface.

When Noam and I interviewed Coralie's former colleagues at SivryMed, it struck me how much they knew about the Yoona situation. They were aware of the protracted love triangle and the suffering it caused everyone involved. They knew Coralie had confronted Yoona, demanding that the young artist leave her nephews alone.

Then there's the matter of Horace's bee venom allergy. Mireille and Nadine knew about it and about Horace's first brush with a bee. Coralie had even shared the doctor's advice that he should avoid getting stung at all costs, because people who react violently the first time, tend to have it even worse the second time.

I stand up and go to the window, deeply distressed by where my thoughts are taking me.

It's clear that Leon and Horace were the center of Coralie's universe, and that she loved to talk about them. If she shared that much with her SivryMed colleagues, including Ines whom she later blackmailed, then it tracks she'd prattle on about Horace and Leon during her regular chiropractic sessions with Quentin.

Quentin would've known about Horace's bee allergy. The chatty Coralie would've brought it up at some point, while he massaged her back. Is it also possible she mentioned something about SivryMed falsifying the trail data? She could've done it inadvertently, when it was still a suspicion, and before they paid for her silence.

The reason why Quentin was never suspected of anything premeditated is that he had nothing to gain and much to lose from Coralie's death.

But what if it isn't so?

What if it was Quentin who killed Coralie, just not how everybody thought? What if it was no tragic accident or malpractice leading to manslaughter, but a cold-blooded, premeditated murder?

What if Quentin also masterminded Horace's death by bees?

But why? What would be his motive?

I can't see any. Just because he had the means and the opportunity to kill two people doesn't mean he did it. He could, of course, be a psychopath choosing from his clientele a random person and family to torment. Or maybe he hated them due to some ancient feud that had started five generations back. Another possibility is that Paul and Ines had hired him to do their dirty work.

I feel I'm getting closer to an important insight. It's right there in front of me, staring me in the face.

As if trying to spot it, I peer at the environment outside the shop. Karl isn't around. I can only hope he's now sitting on a bench next to the little free library in the municipal park, reading. Now that he can, he's tried three different books but, by his own admission, getting back into the habit of reading isn't easy.

The former bistro across the street is under renovation. Beefy men in coveralls tread in, carrying equipment, pipes or metal rods. Other beefy men come out, bent under the weight of large dusty sacks filled with rubble. While most shops are closed today and rue de l'Andouillette almost empty, it's a regular workday for the builders.

As my gaze travels farther down the street, I lose focus. My thoughts return to the Coralie Bray case, and I remember something else. The day after Noam and I visited SivryMed, I was talking on the phone with Quentin. I told him how fishy Ines and Paul had been, and about the SivryPack side effects bombshell that Noam had dropped. Quentin and I ended up dissing the pharmaceutical industry and how drugs are as much cure as poison.

Quentin gave me an example... He said, "Take the Nardil that killed Coralie".

How did he know it was that particular drug and not another with similar effects? Until Sophia named it during our confidential meeting, all I had from Anjara was the name of a class of drugs called MAOIs. He never gave me the specific name, and I doubt he'd have given it to Quentin. It's even less likely that Sophia would've given it to Quentin. They've never even met, as far as I know.

From whom then did Quentin hear about the Nardil in Coralie's blood?

Easy, Julie!

Don't get carried away. Quentin is a health professional, so it's no surprise he'd know the name of the drug. Maybe it's the most common MAOI, or maybe it's the one you can get without a prescription, so he assumed it would be the one the killer had given to Coralie.

FERJ will need to conduct more research. Malvina, Igor's ex, is a pharmacist. We could call her and ask for her expertise. The worst thing we can do now is jump to conclusions and blame an innocent man! An innocent man who trusts me, and for whose benefit we've been investigating this messy case.

Early on, we thought that his choice of Dubai was strange for a penniless man, but FERJ cleared him. We established it was Quentin's parents who'd sponsored his stay there.

Hold on a sec...

The day Salman and I bumped into Quentin in the mall, we talked at one point about the Rapp brothers, and myself, losing a parent too young. Quentin sympathized. He described the hole it had left in his own life—a hole he'd felt particularly keenly during his formative years.

Except, both his mom and dad are still alive. Why would he say such a thing then?

Maybe he was talking about a beloved grandma or a grandpa who had been like a parent to him. *Yes, of course, that's it!* I blame my conspiracy-seeking mind, exasperated that this case is still far from over and for playing tricks on me by casting aspersions on a good man.

Why would Quentin poison Coralie? Or kill Horace whom he'd never even met? What did he stand to gain from those deaths? Nothing! After Coralie died, her money, both the honestly earned and the blackmailed, went to her nephews.

Besides, it's unlikely that Quentin knew about Coralie's side hustle and extra income. Horace was the only person who did. Even Leon didn't know about it. Why on earth would she open up to Quentin?

Again, having the means and the opportunity to kill means nothing without a credible motive. Quentin had none. No motive, no murder.

Suddenly, I feel terrible for focusing on Quentin and disregarding the villainous elephant in the room. His name is Paul Sivry. He may get away with a double homicide. And what can this amateur sleuth do in response when she likes her investigations wrapped as prettily as her pastries, with ribbons tied and curled? She's splitting hairs and trying to find fault with a victim by recasting him as the perpetrator.

Shame on you, Julie Cavallo!

Sometimes I wish I were made differently. I wish I could be exactly what the label says: a gluten-free pastry chef, and nothing more.

Hating myself, I pick up the phone and call Sophia. "I have one last favor to ask of you."

"Ask away."

"Can you look into Quentin Vernet's parents for me? Just the basic facts."

There's a surprised pause, then she says, "I'll call you as soon as it's done."

CHAPTER 29

Too agitated, I struggle more than usual to finish the books today. At around seven, I lower the security gate to avoid distractions. It's ten when I finally finish, and I reopen the gate to a dark and eerily quiet street. Slinging my handbag over my shoulder, I unlock the door.

The moment I open it, a masked man pounces on me and pushes me back into the shop.

I try to scream for help, but he gags me expertly. He's thin and not much taller than me, but he's surprisingly strong. I reach for the safety alarm in my purse. A gloved fist hits me under the ribs, hard. The blow rocks me. Searing pain explodes in my stomach and ripples through my body. I lose my balance and fall to my knees, the alarm slipping from my hand. He kicks it away. Then he grabs my purse. I put up a fight despite the pain. But he absorbs my kicks and punches, wincing at best. He holds me down and retrieves the security gate remote, which he uses immediately to lower the gate.

Damn my love of electronics! If I'd kept my old manual

gate, the one that got stuck more often than it didn't, I would've been so much better off right now.

Once the gate is all the way down, he shoves me onto a chair and ties me to it.

I hate being gagged.

I hate being tied.

I hate that this keeps happening to me, and that I have only myself to blame for it.

He still hasn't said a word. What is he planning to do with me? Is he going to kill me?

My phone rings in my purse.

The masked man—I'm pretty sure it's Regis Chouquet—pulls it out. My lock screen says "Lieutenant Sophia Firmin." *What a fool I am!* When Sophia got her promotion, I was so happy and proud for her I added "lieutenant" to her contact details in my phone. Now Regis knows a gendarme is trying to reach me. He may accelerate his nefarious plan.

He lets the call go to voicemail.

As soon as Sophia leaves her message, he turns to me. "How do I unlock the phone?"

I give him a hooded stare before shifting my eyes to the gag.

He takes it out and puts a knife to my throat. "Password? Face recognition? Fingerprint?"

"Who are you? Are you Regis Chouquet? What do you want?"

He applies more pressure to the blade. "I'm the one asking questions."

"Face," I breathe out.

He holds the screen up to my face, gags me again the moment the phone is unlocked, and then plays Sophia's vocal message.

OK, so the basic facts, as per your request. Quentin's

> mother is as boring as they come. The interesting thing about his father, Michel Vernet, is that he's Quentin's stepfather. Quentin's real father, Gerard Astier, took his own life thirty-five years ago, when Quentin was eight. A year later, Michel Vernet married Quentin's mom and legally adopted her son, giving the boy his family name. Let me know if want me to dig deeper.

Slanting me a black look, Regis picks up his own phone and calls someone.

"Yes," he says when the other person answers. "I have her. Good thing I do, man! She's onto both of us."

"Both?" I half hear half guess the reaction.

"She just had a lieutenant leave her a voicemail with info about your family."

Quentin says something I can't hear.

"No," Regis says. "Stay where you are for now. I need you on the lookout while I work."

Work. What does he mean by that? Does he mean...?

A shiver runs down my spine and my hands become damp. If only I could reach my purse, and the self-defense knife in it! But it's too far from me. As is the safety alarm. All the protection I'm left with is the evil eye bracelet on my wrist.

Quentin speaks again.

Regis turns red in the face. "I don't care that you're paying me! You should trust my instincts."

They're crap because you got caught three times.

I'm guessing Quentin tells him the same thing, because Regis' face turns burgundy. "Not my problem. It's my face on the BOLO, not yours! You know what? Bring in the bum."

The bum? What bum?

There's a soft rap on the window.

Regis swears under his breath, before reopening the security gate and then the door.

Quentin peeps in. "I need a hand."

Regis checks that my gag and ties will stay in place, picks up the alarm from the floor, and rushes out.

Seconds later, Quentin and Regis reenter, dragging in a limp body. It's Karl. He's alive, but much more spaced out than his norm. They must've drugged him.

What about Harley? He'd be barking his head off now. I can only hope they sedated him, too. But I fear they poisoned him. It's Quentin's MO, after all.

Are they going to kill me the same way?

Regis pulls out his knife again and holds it in a way that signals he's ready to use it.

Quentin picks up the remote and lowers the gate.

Looming over me, he announces in a news anchor's tone, "A tragedy took place in central Beldoc last night. A homeless man known as Karl, high on crack, stabbed to death pastry chef Julie Cavallo in a robbery gone wrong. He then overdosed and died in her shop."

Regis pushes the corners of his mouth down. "Sad. Very sad!"

I stare into Quentin's eyes so hard I'm practically burning a hole in them.

He squats next to me. "I'm going to ungag you, so you can say your piece. But if you scream, we'll hurt you before we kill you. Understand?"

I nod.

He removes the disgusting gag.

"Why?" I ask. "Why are you doing this? Why did you kill Coralie and Horace? What have you gained from it?"

"You're dying to know, aren't you?"

I nod again.

He clicks his tongue. "Well, that's tough, *chérie*. I'm afraid you'll die without knowing."

"What? Why?"

"I'd be happy to fulfill your last wish, but I don't have the time."

I glower at him. "I found the time to get the police to review your case, to reopen the investigation—"

"And I'm grateful. But you should've stopped there."

I knit my brows. "Then I wouldn't've uncovered the evidence incriminating Ines and Paul!"

"True." He glances at Regis. "I'm conflicted, believe me. You've been extremely useful for a while."

Regis steps closer to me. "The problem with you is that you keep digging when others stop, including the cops."

"And the more you dig, the closer you get to us," Quentin says. "You bragged the other day that you'd uncovered some material evidence. What was it? Is that why Regis is suddenly on the Most Wanted list?"

"I found some CCTV footage," I confess, not daring to defy two angry murderers. "Horace had installed a home security system."

Quentin turns the air blue with words so vulgar that I startle. But then I recall he spent a year in jail. *Is that where he met Regis?*

The burglar snarls at me. "Because of you, I'm a fugitive now. I live in hiding, like a rat."

"And I begin to make mistakes," Quentin says.

I shift my gaze to him. "Like when you mentioned the drug, Nardil."

"The word was out before I could stop myself." He shakes his head ruefully. "You didn't catch it right then, but it was only a matter of time until you circled back and realized the implications."

"That explains why you're killing me," I say, doing my

best to remain calm while uttering those words. "But why did you kill Coralie and Horace?"

"Too long to explain, too complex, too personal," he says. "I'll put it all into a single word as a thank you for helping me. Retribution."

"For what?" I ask.

Regis takes another step toward us and gags me again. "OK, that's it! Enough talking—"

A loud knock reverberates in the shop. "Julie! Are you in there? Open up!"

It's Gabriel! I groan and jump up and down with my chair trying to make as much noise as I can.

Regis swears under his breath and glances at Quentin. "What do we do?"

His knife is pointing at me.

Before Quentin gets a chance to answer, Karl lunges for the remote, seizes hold of it and falls to his knees again. Still too groggy to stand, he manages to push the right button. The gate begins to slide up.

Regis jumps on him, stabbing him in the upper back. Karl falls facedown. A dark stain appears on his favorite bomber jacket around the stab wound and spreads out fast. Too fast.

Everything is happening way too fast.

Gabriel wraps his elbow in his jacket and breaks the glass. The shop alarm goes off. He pulls out his gun and shoots. Regis drops to the floor. While the alarm blares into the night, Quentin's hands encircle my throat. I squirm and struggle. It's hard to breathe. Quentin's face is red, distorted with rage. Then it becomes a blur, and the only thing I see is the mole protruding over his right eye. Everything around it fades to black.

Through the darkness, a low hiss begins. It grows louder

until it becomes a familiar crackling noise like television static.

I'm in a hallway, facing a closed interior door. From how quiet and dark everything is, I conclude it's nighttime. I'm small, but I'm attached to something, and I move with that larger thing that I'm attached to. With an effort I focus on my immediate environment.

Is that a... eyelid? Yes. And a nose, and, above me, an eyebrow. I'm attached to somebody's face, between the eye and the eyebrow.

I'm Quentin's raised mole! Except in this snapshot, he's much shorter than in real life, given that I'm only twenty or so centimeters above the doorknob he's staring at.

Am I in his childhood? How old is he? Based on his height, I'd say eight or nine. No more than ten, for sure.

Is he going to open that door?

What's behind it?

Quentin tiptoes closer to the door. From the way he angles and tilts his head, I'm guessing he's decided to eavesdrop rather than go in.

I focus on the sounds. Behind the door, a man and a woman are arguing in hushed voices.

"You're their fall guy," the woman says. "They've turned all your colleagues against you, even your friends."

"Sylvaine, don't—" the man begins.

"Don't what?" she cuts him off. "Call it as it is? That your beloved, trusted boss has made a scapegoat of you to protect his own reputation?"

"Sylvaine—" he says again.

"What, Gerard?" she hisses, interrupting him again. "It's the truth."

Gerard? As in Gerard Astier, Quentin's real dad who died thirty-five years ago?

"It isn't the whole truth," he says.

"All of them." she jumps in again, too mad to let him contradict her. "From Didier to the site manager to that chatty young secretary, they're all happy to sacrifice you to save the company and their jobs."

"The whole truth is that it was me operating the crane when it swayed." There's a fraught silence before he adds, "It was my hand that took two young lives."

"Bullshit," she hisses. "That crane was too old, too wobbly. You'd told the site manager about it. Didier himself had been informed. But they wouldn't listen!"

"The manager did listen," Gerard corrects her. "It was Didier that chose to wait before replacing it."

"And now they're both denying you'd ever raised the matter with them," she spits out. "Didier even got an expert to certify the crane was in the clear!"

"What if it was?" Gerard asks, his voice coarse and his tone defeated. "Maybe I'm the only one to blame for what happened. Not the company equipment. Not Didier Sivry. Just me."

Before I can hear Sylvaine's answer, the darkness in the apartment thickens. It swaddles me tight and swallows me whole.

CHAPTER 30

Gabriel, Commissaire Anjara, and I are roaming the small but delightful Summer Garden of Arles. Located between the commissariat and the Roman theater and leaning against the medieval city wall, the park rolls down a hillside to the Boulevard des Lices. Initially, Gabriel and I were supposed to see Anjara in his office, but he suggested we take a walk instead. I breathe in the fragrant air still fresh from the night and decide that this is a great idea.

A week has passed since Quentin Vernet and his accomplice Regis Chouquet broke into my shop and tried to murder Karl and me. In the end, Regis was the one that didn't make it out alive.

All the other protagonists survived.

Quentin suffered a concussion from the blow to the head he received from Gabriel while trying to strangle me. I got away with bruising on my neck and wrists, a few scrapes, and another blackout. Karl lost a lot of blood. Luckily, no vital organs were damaged. Gabriel was able to stem the bleeding, and then help arrived. Karl is now being treated at the hospital.

Harley is camping in Rose's garden.

Instead of killing the dog, Quentin had given him a treat laced with a sedative. Since Harley became Rose's guest, she's hosed him down and washed him in Lady's inflatable pool, but she still won't let him inside the house or near Lady. Sarah, on the other hand, is happy for her pug Baxter to fraternize with Harley. She hopes that making friends with a male dog will help Baxter switch back to raising a leg instead of squatting when he pees.

Leon Rapp was fully cleared and released from custody.

"This is my favorite place in the entire town," Anjara says as we ascend a purely decorative horseshoe-shaped staircase that arches over a romantic basin with vines, a fountain, and rocaille.

"Why is it called a summer garden?" I ask him.

"It was established in the nineteenth century as a counterpoint to Winter Garden on the other side of the Boulevard des Lices." Smiling at my confused face, he adds, "Winter Garden is long gone, but this one survived."

We pass an uncluttered, discreet stele.

Gabriel halts and touches its limestone surface, visibly moved. "How did I not know about this memorial?"

"Few people do," Anjara says.

Before I can read the text engraved on the stele, Gabriel moves on. I follow, struck once again by how little he talks about himself, his family, and his roots. Whether it's out of a misguided *pudeur*, or to protect them or just because opening up isn't in his nature, it stings a bit.

Perhaps with time, I tell myself. Seeing as it took him a year and a half to kiss me, I can reasonably expect to visit the barracks where he lives in a couple of years, and then to meet his parents in a decade or so. Perhaps he'll be ready to start a family of his own after he retires from active duty.

Will it be too late for me by then?

To take my mind off those depressing musings, I turn to Anjara. "That gut feeling you had about Quentin the first time around turned out to be right, after all."

"Yeah... except I'd misinterpreted it as medical malpractice and not premeditated murder."

"Nobody could've suspected it at the time," Gabriel says.

"There wasn't a hint of a motive," I join in. "Has he confessed?"

"Not only did he confess, but he's fully cooperating with the investigation."

Anjara's reply makes me stop in my tracks. "Really?"

"Of course, Madame! In exchange, the magistrates and the detectives have assured him that Paul Sivry will face the full severity of the law, despite his money and connections."

Gabriel looks me in the eye. "This morning, I was authorized to tell you that a criminal investigation is being launched into Paul Sivry, Ines Kabbaj, and their company on the basis of the documents you found in that gym locker."

I clap my hands and we resume the walk.

"Would you like to know what Quentin's motive was?" Anjara asks me. "When he was eight, his father, Gerard Astier, operated a crane for a construction company owned by Didier Sivry, Paul Sivry's father."

I already figured that out from my snapshot, but I do my best not to show it.

"The crane fell, killing two workers," Anjara continues. "Didier Sivry and his company were cleared of any responsibility. Gerard Astier was facing manslaughter charges. He committed suicide even before he was indicted."

Again, I already know that, from Sophia this time, but I'm obviously not going to mention it.

"I'm assuming Quentin's mother remarried," I say instead. "And the stepfather adopted the boy."

Anjara inclines his head as a sign of appreciation. "Your sleuthing truly is as good as they say!"

I avert my gaze, ashamed he thinks I figured it out on my own, when I just learned it from Sophia.

"Quentin's mother always told him his dad had been innocent," Anjara carries on. "In his teens, he vowed to avenge him one day."

"Why didn't he then go after Didier?" I ask.

"Didier Sivry died fifteen years after the events," Anjara says. "His son Paul sold the construction business and reinvested in his pharma start-up, SivryMed."

"And so, Quentin transferred his hunger for revenge to Paul," I infer.

"Correct."

A question I meant to ask a few minutes ago resurfaces in my mind. "How did Gerard Astier kill himself?"

"Pills," Anjara says. "A massive overdose."

I level my gaze with Anjara's. "Basically, he poisoned himself."

"Yes. And that's one of the reasons Quentin chose that method to dispatch Coralie Bray."

I knit my eyebrows. "I don't get it. Why didn't he poison Didier's son, Paul? Why kill a lowly PA that hadn't wronged his father in any way?"

"Not quite," Anjara says. "In her youth, Coralie Bray was Didier's secretary. According to Quentin's mom, Coralie owed Gerard a big favor, but she didn't hesitate to turn her back on him after the tragic accident."

The chatty young secretary Sylvaine mentioned in my snapshot was Coralie!

Anjara points out a tree. "That's an Asian magnolia by the way. And that one is a Lebanese cedar."

"They're beautiful."

"And that one, over there, is a Japanese ginkgo biloba." He grins. "It's a plant equivalent of a crocodile, barely evolved since the Jurassic."

"The crocodiles have shrunk though," Gabriel remarks.

Anjara's grin widens. "Thank God!"

My thoughts return to Quentin's motives. "Still," I say, "Coralie was just a secretary. Doesn't killing her instead of Paul turn the whole vendetta theme into a farce?"

"Coralie's poisoning wasn't an end in itself, but a means toward an end," Anjara says. "Quentin didn't want to kill Paul. He wanted to make him miserable, ruined, disgraced, accused of fraud and of murder, abandoned by everyone—"

I gasp. "He wanted Paul to kill himself!"

He nods. "Six years ago, Quentin learned that Paul had hired Coralie as a PA for Ines Kabbaj. He found out Coralie had back issues, and he made sure she heard about his talents in that area."

Slowly, I lift my chin. "Wow, that's some premeditation!"

"He was able to relieve her pain," Anjara continues. "Coralie became a regular. Her talking nonstop about herself and her nephews was an unexpected bonus."

I tilt my head to one side. "That's how he learned about Horace's allergy, right?"

"Right."

"Was that also how he found out about the fraud with the SivryPack drug trial?" Gabriel asks Anjara. "Was Coralie stupid enough to tell him while taking Paul's hush money?"

"She never told him about it," Anjara says. "But she often used his Wi-Fi in the waiting room. All Quentin had to do was pay a hacker to gain remote access to her phone and install a spy app on it."

My mouth drops. "I didn't know you could do that!"

"A word of advice?" Anjara gives me a mischievous smile. "Don't think of your phone as a private device that will keep your secrets."

"From this day on, I never will."

Gabriel turns to Anjara. "You mentioned that Quentin wanted Paul Sivry accused of murder, among other things. Was he hoping to pin Coralie's death on Paul?"

"Indeed, he expected the police would treat Coralie's death as murder, and the investigation would lead to Paul who had a major motive—Coralie's blackmail."

Gabriel winks. "Except that's not quite how it unfolded."

"I went after Quentin instead." Anjara spreads his hands. "What can I say? Quentin's stars lost their alignment. The ME mucked up his report and missed the probable cause of the stroke. I was hell-bent on my medical malpractice theory. Horace ignored Quentin's letter."

"What letter?" Gabriel and I ask in unison.

"The one he'd sent anonymously, from a colleague of Coralie's," Anjara says. "In it, he insinuated that SivryMed benefited from Coralie's death, and urged the Rapp brothers to demand additional tests and a second opinion from another ME. He also strongly suggested they search the house for any damning SivryMed files."

"Had Leon seen that letter?" I ask.

"Quentin couldn't've known it at the time but no, he hadn't," Anjara replies. "Horace must've destroyed it after reading."

Gabriel rubs at his neck. "That's consistent with Horace's character, and with the fact he later decided to blackmail SivryMed himself."

We fall silent as Gabriel and I process what we've just learned, and Anjara gives us time to do it. My gaze travels from the beautiful ruins of the Roman theater outside the park to the marble statue of a mythology-inspired woman in front of us.

"Niobe, daughter of Tantalus," Anjara says.

I study her face. "She seems upset."

"I used to know why…" Anjara screws up his face. "For the life of me, can't remember it now… Was it betrayal? Undeserved punishment? Murder of a loved one?"

"Antique tragedy had it all, didn't it?" Gabriel says.

Anjara nods, glancing from him to me. "Ready for the second act of our modern tragedy?"

"Yes," Gabriel says.

I let Anjara assume I am. The truth, however, is that I'm not at all ready. And I'm not certain I'll be ready in five minutes, or in five days. I'm the kind of girl that would never pick up a book or watch a movie that doesn't end happily. I bake sweets for a living. Whenever life takes a bad turn, I try to find something positive about it.

If it weren't for Mom's death, I wouldn't be investigating murders in my free time.

That, I am quite certain of.

CHAPTER 31

Magda steps into Igor's nearly ready bookshop, dressed in a brand-new silky gown, her highlights redone and her nails manicured. She has a lollipop in her mouth. Since she quit smoking last Monday, she's been sucking on one nonstop. They help her combat her nicotine cravings.

The rest of us are already gathered around the builder's workbench that we've moved to the center. Igor expects to open for business a week from now. Magda will need another week. She's still looking for a shop assistant capable of upselling as masterfully as she does. I'm afraid she'll have to lower the bar if Lavender Dream 2 is to ever open its door to customers.

She says to Igor, "I didn't realize you had so many friends in Beldoc!"

"Julie, Eric and I put together this dessert buffet to celebrate two things." Igor leads her to the workbench. "My upcoming opening, and the completion of FERJ's latest case."

Nudging Sarah away so she can squeeze herself next to

Igor, Magda surveys the guests once again. "I don't see the man that was released from prison thanks to FERJ."

"Leon left just five minutes ago," Yoona, on my right, says. "He's very busy, because Pretty Pooch of Provence is reopening on Tuesday."

Eric pours Magda a glass of Ponsards' muscatel.

She raises it. "To openings, reopenings, and new beginnings!"

Everybody cheers and drinks to that.

I swear, my relief that I'm no longer on Magda's hit list is as great as my pride that we cracked the case.

From his wheelchair, Karl points at the empty shelves. "Once they're filled with books, this place will become the beating heart of rue de l'Andouillette."

Magda and I begin to protest that the street already has a heart and that it's our respective shops, when Igor intervenes, "It will be the literary heart."

Nice damage control, buddy!

Magda and I shut up, appeased.

"That's what I meant to say," Karl throws Magda and me a guilty look. "My social skills are rusty."

One day when I have time, I'll sit down with him and make him tell me about his life before the streets. And if he refuses, then I'll investigate. His heroic action saved my life —both of our lives—on that fateful night, but that's no reason to spare him my busybody ways.

That being said, I do intend to show him my gratitude. And the first thing I've done was to find a leather jacket identical to Karl's fetish garment that Regis had ruined. I ordered it online three days ago. It should be delivered tomorrow.

Giving up hope there'll be scraps, Harley leaves Karl's side by the workbench and trots to the window. There on the hard floor, Lady and Baxter are stretched out on their tummies in a yellow rectangular painted by the afternoon sun. Their eyes are closed in bliss as their spirits roam Doggie Nirvana. What with the walls and the ceiling still damp, it's too cool inside Igor's shop for a dog's comfort. That explains Harley's migration. He joins the sunbathers, grunting with pleasure.

"You must sample Julie's new macarons! They're to die for," Igor says to Magda.

She points at the lollipop in her mouth. "As soon as I'm done with this."

"You missed the first part of the FERJ report," he says. "Would you like me to give you a recap while we wait?"

She moves closer to him. "Absolutely. But why are we waiting?"

"Julie's sisters Veronique and Catherine, and her friend Salman, were with us via video call," he explains. "They had to step away for an hour."

With that, he launches into a whispered summary, and Magda gives him her undivided attention.

I murmur to Yoona, "Is it true what a little bird told me?"

The little bird is Flo, who was still surveilling Yoona as late as last week, fascinated by the woman's art and her personality. She swears she's stopped as of this week.

"That Leon and I are engaged?" Yoona's lips curve up. "Yes. While he was in jail, I realized he's my true love, and so I proposed to him."

"And he said yes?"

She lowers her eyelids. "On the condition there will never be another triangle."

"So, you think it's doable?" I wait for her to lift her gaze. "You think Leon will be enough now, when he wasn't before?"

"You know what drew me to him after I'd started dating Horace?"

"What?" I pick up a *panna cotta*.

"His incredible generosity. It swept me off my feet." She winks. "A bit like you and your gendarme."

I freeze with my spoon halfway to my mouth.

Yoona giggles at my reaction. "You aren't in a hurry to go public with it, are you?"

I refuse to confirm her guess, but I don't want to lie either, so I simply say nothing.

She purrs, "You told us earlier that Capitaine Adinian had returned to Beldoc on Monday night instead of Tuesday morning, because he'd sensed you were in danger."

Is that what gave me away? With a nod, I bring the spoon to my mouth.

"Only a fool would've missed the glow in your eyes." Yoona's expression becomes dreamy. "I have a similar bond with Leon. We had it from the moment we met."

"Yet, you went back to Horace," I point out.

"Thing is..." She plays with a lock of her hair, looking for the right words. "At the time, Leon was too naïve, too guileless for an adult. He was a man-child, not a man."

"And now?"

"The events of the past weeks have transformed him, Julie! He's a man now." A silvery laugh escapes her lips. "And our dynamic is completely different."

"How so?"

"He doesn't look up to me all the time, like he used to. He doesn't expect me to always take the lead. We've become equals."

"Careful what you wish for," I tease her. "You may come to miss the pedestal."

"I doubt that very much."

"Aha?"

"What happened is he stopped needing me to fill his late mother's shoes. Why would I miss that?"

My phone rings. It's Salman. I turn the video on and prop my phone against a jar so that he can see as much as possible. Within minutes, Vero is back on Flo's screen, and Cat on Rose's.

"I have a question," Vero says. "When Quentin learned about the falsified trial results, why didn't he take that scoop to the press? It was his chance to get back at Paul Sivry."

"I've been wondering the same thing," Salman joins in, "when I wasn't wondering how he'd deceived me for years into thinking he was a good person."

"He deceived me, too," I console him.

"It worked so well, because a good part of his story was true," Rose offers. "And because he was sincere in his feeling of victimhood."

Salman's mouth twists into a grimace. "Yeah, he just chose to leave a pile of dead bodies as stepping stones to his revenge."

"Commissaire Anjara asked Quentin that same question," I say.

"And?"

"Quentin explained that, first, he didn't have any material proof beyond his illegally hacking Coralie's conversations with Ines Kabbaj, the head of R & D."

On Flo's screen, Vero frowns. "It was still a big scoop…"

"Quentin feared Paul would bribe the local and national press to ax the story," I say. "Or that he'd bribe officials to order the press to ax the story."

"Ha!" Cat cries out from Rose's phone. "Didn't Marie-Jo shelve the interview you and Noam did at SivryMed? Grandma told me about it."

"Marie-Jo was made to do it," I confirm. "And anyway, even if a brave newspaper had written about the fraud and a police investigation confirmed it, Quentin was certain Paul would avoid prosecution."

"How?" Cat asks.

"The way his father had gotten away with it thirty-five years ago," Salman answers in my stead. "By shifting the responsibility on an employee such as Ines Kabbaj."

Igor strokes his mustache. "It's not like she didn't know what she was doing, did she?"

"Oh, she was totally in on it," I say.

Yoona's face contorts with anger. "I hope they both rot in jail for the lives they've taken!"

"And the lives they've ruined with their drug that should've never been approved," Magda adds.

I clap to get everyone focused. "Back to the case, or else we'll never be done. So, by sacrificing Coralie, a pawn in his game, Quentin hoped to make sure Paul didn't get away."

"But things didn't work out quite the way he'd planned them," Eric prompts.

"No, they didn't," I concur. "Instead of avenging his aunt, Horace chose to relaunch her blackmail scheme. As a result, Quentin spent a year in jail for medical malpractice and three months in Dubai to regroup before he returned to France with a new plan."

"To punish Horace," Yoona bites out.

"To punish both Rapp brothers by killing one and getting the other convicted for it," I correct her. "He didn't know Leon was in the dark."

"And that brings me to the second thing I've been racking my brain about," Vero jumps in. "Why didn't Quentin and that burglar he met in jail, Regis, just stage the same kind of murder and suicide they almost pulled off with Julie and Karl?"

Karl shivers in his wheelchair and spills his wine.

While Rose dabs his shirt with napkins, I refill his glass.

"Bee venom isn't a very reliable murder method, is it?" I add.

"But it's creative," Flo counters. "The plan was ingenious if you think about it. Regis breaks in at dawn, just before Horace goes for a jog. He steals the EpiPen from Horace's backpack and plants it in Leon's trash. Then he puts on a mask and a blond wig in case there are eyewitnesses and unleashes the bees on Horace."

"That plan worked better, by the way, than the more banal approach they later tried with Julie and Karl," Yoona says. "Horace died and Leon was indicted."

I touch her arm sympathetically. "At the time, we all thought Leon had killed Horace and made it look like an accident."

"We also thought he was dumb," Flo chimes in, as tactful as ever. "Who steals their victim's life-saving EpiPen and tosses it in their own trash?"

"That's because Quentin wanted Horace's death to look suspicious," I remind her. "He wanted it to look like premeditated murder posing as an accident."

A silence ensues while my friends are digesting my convoluted statement.

"I have a toast!" Igor announces.

Everybody raises their glass.

He draws in a breath. "To justice, to perseverance, and to always keeping a cool head!"

"What I've learned from this past month," Salman says, "is to question every story I'm fed, by anyone, always."

"Remember the bird drifting downstream on a twig?" Eric asks me.

"When we picnicked on the Rhône?" I incline my head. "You said you shared its life philosophy."

He beams at me. "Not anymore! From now on, I'd rather swim against the current."

"My dear boy," Rose says. "The point isn't to swim against the current for the sake of it."

"It's much easier to go where the current takes you," Karl interjects.

Rose cocks her head. "Does the current give a damn about you? How do you know it isn't taking you straight to the falls?"

"I guess I don't know," Karl concedes.

Magda rubs at her forehead. "What is it you're trying to tell us, Rose?"

"Hard rules are for fools," she states. "There are times to drift downstream, times to swim against the current, and times when crossing the river is the best way forward."

"Is that the motto you live by?" Igor asks her.

"The non-drifting options are hard, and it isn't obvious what the best course is," she concedes. "But I always try."

My sisters and I exchange looks. Despite our many differences, each of us marches to the beat of her own drum.

Whoever could've taught us that?

AUTHOR'S NOTE

Dear Reader,

I hope you enjoyed **The Bloodthirsty Bee!**

To help other readers discover my work, and to encourage me to continue the series, please consider leaving a brief review.

It's easy. Just go to the book's Amazon page, scroll down and click "Write a review"!

Goodreads is another great place to share your thoughts about my books.

Thank you!
Ana

FREE RECIPE BOOK

Sign up for my monthly newsletter and receive a free cookbook in your inbox!

The quick and easy gluten-free recipes in it include:

- macarons
- cookies
- brownies
- tiramisu
- fritters
- puddings, and more!

To sign up, type this url into your browser:
ana-drew.com/patissier

ABOUT THE AUTHOR

Ana T. Drew is the evil mastermind behind the recent series of murders in the fictional French town of Beldoc.

When she is not writing cozy mysteries or doing mom-and-wife things, she can be found watching "The Rookie" to help her get over "Castle".

She lives in Paris but her heart is in Provence.

∼

Website: ana-drew.com

- amazon.com/author/ana-drew
- facebook.com/AnaDrewAuthor
- goodreads.com/anadrew
- bookbub.com/authors/ana-t-drew

ALSO BY ANA T. DREW

The Canceled Christmas
(novella)

THE JULIE CAVALLO INVESTIGATES SERIES

The Murderous Macaron

The Killer Karma

The Sinister Superyacht

The Shady Chateau

The Perils of Paris

The Bloodthirsty Bee

Printed in Great Britain
by Amazon